Family & Lies

SARA FAYAZ

First Published in January 2022

ISBN: 978-93-93809-77-3

BLUEROSE PUBLISHERS

www.bluerosepublishers.com

info@bluerosepublishers.com

+91 8882 898 898

Cover Design:

Geetika Kandari

Typographic Design:

Pooja Sharma

Distributed by: BlueRose, Amazon, Flipkart

Acknowledgments

First and foremost, I want to thank my Lord Almighty who has given me everything and more. I can never find the words to express my gratitude (which says a lot being an author) to my parents who have always been by my side no matter what. They're the embodiment of inspiration. They have inspired me to write this book. I couldn't have done it without them. I'm forever grateful to my siblings; Sufyaan, Omar and Khadija. Sufyaan has been my greatest audience listening to my endless rants about how I had writer's block, to Omar who continually encouraged me telling I was doing great and finally Khadija who kept me going with her little babbles. Also, I want to thank my grandparents who have been forever supportive and pampered me with all their love.

Dedication

To Myself.

There are way too many people who I want to dedicate my book to so instead of going through the torture of picking one person I dedicated this book to myself.

Author Introduction

Sara Fayaz is a home-schooled teenager. She's a science nerd who loves literature and uses music to disconnect from the world. She's the eldest of her four siblings and her family means the world to her.

As a child she always dreamed of being an author. She has competed in numerous elocution competitions and secured first place almost every time. She loves experimenting with different writing styles.

Family & Lies is her first fully completed book, which might just have a sequel.

PART-1

Chapter-1

FLASHBACK

Hey, I am Lee Nayeon a 15-year-old living the perfect life. I just came back home after shopping for 4 hours straight. And the best part is I went with my best friend, we bought designer outfits to wear for Minjee's birthday party. Choi Minjee is my best friend and we have been friends for the past 6 years. We are inseparable but there's one thing that can change that, if she found out about my dad's work, she would abandon me and so would all my other friends. But I wouldn't blame them for leaving me, if my friend's dad was a mafia, I would fear them too. But I'm sure no one's going to find out anytime soon, I was brought out of my thoughts when my maid asked me if I was going to shower and have dinner or wanted my dinner first, "I already had dinner with Minjee, so I think I'll just go and take a shower" I replied nodding, she left. So, I left my bags there so my maid could bring it to my room later. I then went up to my room and picked out a nice pair of pajamas to wear after my shower, I walked into the bathroom, switched the faucet on and watched as hot, steaming water flowed into the tub, before I realized, the tub was full, so I peeled off my clothes and got in, the hot water giving me goosebumps. Once I finished my bath and got dressed, I got on my bed and started scrolling through Instagram until I found something that caught my eye, it was a pair of gorgeous white heeled boots with ragged edges at the bottom soles; it looked like it was made to match the dress I had bought for Minjee's party. So, I went ahead and ordered it online. It would come in two days which was perfect considering the party was in two days, but it only started at midnight so I would get the shoes in the morning and wear it at night. It had already gotten late, and dad is supposed to come back from his trip early in the morning and I wanted to be awake before he arrives so I could make him his favourite snack, chocolate chip cookies. Mom used to bake this for us whenever dad got back home from his trips. It's been almost 3 years since mom passed away it was something very unexpected since she was as healthy as ever when she passed away and so I still can't seem to bring up the topic in front of dad, he is still recovering from the shock. It took a really long time for me to get used to the fact that she was gone too but I have slowly but surely learned that there's nothing I can do about it. I still break down a lot when I think about her it's really hard but I have to stay strong for dad, he might be the leader of a huge gang of mafias but he still has a heart. I kept thinking about mom and ended up falling asleep.

I woke up by the sound of my alarm going off. I opened my eyes and sat up, I picked up my phone to check the time, it's currently 6:00AM and I have two hours before dad gets home. I hurry and do my morning routine which consists of minimal things like washing my face, brushing my teeth, moisturizing and brushing through my tangled hair. As I got out of the toilet I got into my enormous closet and picked out a denim skirt which had threads hanging loose at the bottom, I paired it with a top and a denim jacket which complimented the skirt. After getting dressed I went downstairs and headed to the kitchen. Our house is pretty big even though it's just me and my dad who stay here with our maids and helpers. I reached the kitchen and started getting the batter ready for the cookies. Once I was done, I heated the oven and poured the batter into the cookie mould, I had picked out a heart shaped mould. I then put the cookie mould in the oven and headed to the living room I got my laptop out to see what my first class was, well I am being home-schooled since the time mom passed away because I wanted to be there for dad and also because apparently not having a mother is a great reason to bully someone. So, after checking my mail I found out that my first class is math and I absolutely hate math so I decided I would rather skip this class. Just as I was mailing my teacher, I heard the bell ring that meant dad was home after a long week away. So, I sprinted to the door and opened it, dad saw me and smiled, looking at him my lips tugged up into a big smile, I gave him a big hug, the both of us walked into living room before one of our maids came and took dad's bag to his room, just as he sat down, I told him that I had a surprise for him. I raced to the kitchen, the cookies were still warm so I carefully placed them on a plate and carried it to the living room walking backwards. I did a 180 degree turn and held the tray in front of dad's face laughing at my childish behaviour he picked one up before slowly taking a big bite, almost finishing the whole cookie in one bite. He chewed slowly before his eyes lit up, his lips displayed a proud smile but in a moment his smile had turned into a frown and his cheerful expression dropped, I couldn't tell what was wrong I followed mom's instructions precisely but what I hadn't realised was the fact that, that was exactly the problem, I hesitantly asked dad what was wrong worry lacing my words. "These tastes just like the ones your mother used to make" he mumbled, "that's because I followed her recipe, I thought it would be a nice surprise" I replied. "Thank you Nay" he replied, not knowing what to say I just nodded. I then tried to change the subject and tell him about Minjee's birthday the day after tomorrow, I spoke to him about the theme we picked together and then I showed him the diamond chocker I got her to match her dress for the party as her gift. We then spoke about how the past week had been for both of us and then dad realized that it would be time for my class very soon, so I told him that I cancelled today's class because he was coming. He wasn't mad so I was relieved. He said that he didn't have any work today so we could go out for ice cream and binge watch some movies after he got changed, I agreed and just as dad was walking up the stairs, I had a sharp pain in my head and I fainted for the third time this week. Dad darted towards me and pulled me into his arms while called for the maid, who came rushing towards us with a glass of water to sprinkle on my face. And I had come back to my senses. Dad was very worried, he asked me if I was alright, I didn't want to tell him that this had happened before and worry him more, so instead I said, "I'm fine, it's probably because I slept late last night and woke up early, I think I just need some rest." "Ok but please don't push yourself so hard next time, you could've just made the cookies in the evening, never mind just go to your room and take a little nap, Aecha please accompany her to her room in case she feels lightheaded again or wait should I sit next to you as you sleep so that way, I can keep an eye on you" dad was mumbling incoherently with worry. So, to reassure him I said, "Dad again, I'm fine Aecha will accompany me to my room, so you don't worry I won't be out of her sight, you just got back from a week-long trip so take some rest you need it more," slightly yelling the last part as I was already half way up the stairs. With a worried sigh dad climbed the stairs following in my footsteps and walked into his room letting us walk further into the house to my room. I got into my room with Aecha following suite, I sat on the bed and there was a moment of silence in between us. The silence was broken by my maid who asked me if I had remembered something else and I told her that this time I had seen myself, running into a busy road to save a small girl who was probably around 3 years old and I kept calling her Aecha, Kim Aecha. And then a truck came our way I pushed her away, but I couldn't save myself and the truck crashed into me. This has been happening for the past week. I would see something like a flashback and I would see different events each time. But it couldn't be me as I would be wearing worn out clothes and I had a sister and the people I called my parents were not my mom and dad. When I told my maid about this, she told me that it could have been my past life, which I agree, sounds totally stupid but I don't know what else it could mean. At first, I thought she was probably saying stuff like this because she's just eighteen and has always been interested in weird stuff like this. But it seems like she was right all along because I just saw myself dying. I'm not sure what to think anymore. I told her, "I just want to take a little nap, this is all too much to process and I probably need some sleep anyways. I'm sure you have better things to do than watch me sleep so why don't you go ahead and finish up any other work you have." After she left, I picked up my phone and clicked on the icon with multi-coloured G, I was beyond curious now I needed to know if there are actually instances where people remember their past lives so I searched it up and apparently, it's a pretty common occurrence though not all of them are real, there were some pretty convincing incidents. Now I really needed to shut my eyes for a while, so I can just take in everything I learned, a lot had happened this past week. Just pondering on what every little detail could mean I fell asleep.

I was woken up by someone gently stroking my hair, dad was trying to wake me up because it turns out I had slept through lunch and now it was time for dinner and dad was worried because I hadn't even eaten a proper breakfast. So, I got out of bed went to the bathroom washed my face to get rid of the sleep in my eyes and tied my hair into a ponytail. Then I headed downstairs and went to the dining room where dad was seated on the dining table, the food had already been served but he was waiting for me. Pulling out the chair I sat down, and without a word we both started eating. Both of us have this habit of focusing solely on our food when we eat which was something mom had enforced on us. We would eat our food in silence and sit together to play a game, watch a movie or just talk to each other after our dinner. That's why I was a little startled when dad asked me how I'm feeling. I told him that I was feeling much better now and that I was probably just tired. Then I asked him if he was still up for ice cream and k-dramas tomorrow. But he said that he couldn't spend time with me tomorrow as he had to head to work early in the morning, I was a little heartbroken that I had messed today up and that I couldn't spend time with him tomorrow. He most definitely understood that by my pouting lips and sad demeanour, and so he told me that we could still go out on a short drive and get some ice cream if I finished my food quickly. Smiling happily, I hurriedly started stuffing food down my throat almost choking twice. As soon as I was done dad got the car keys, I grabbed my denim jacket, which I had taken off earlier and headed out. It was pretty chilly out tonight. We both got into the car and dad asked me where I wanted to go, I told him that we should go to the one nearby since their cookies and cream flavoured ice-cream is heavenly. Both of us jammed to music the whole way and back, singing along at an obnoxiously loud volume which is most probably considered yelling. By the time we reached home it was pretty late, so we decided to go to bed.

The next morning, I woke up quite late since I didn't have any classes today, I had cancelled them all because I was going to go to Minjee's place so we could spend some time with each other before we get ready for the party together. I took a shower and put on an almost full black outfit consisting of a green turtle neck which was tucked into my high waist black jeans, a black knee length winter jacket and a black beret to top it all off. I had straightened my long naturally wavy hair today, leaving it loose under my beret, leaving my bangs on my forehead. I then put on a little bit of foundation and a simple lipstick since I had to take it off later for the party. I then went to have my breakfast as I sat to have my breakfast my maid told me that dad had already left for work, I just nodded and continued eating. After I had finished my breakfast, I went and packed a bag with my dress for the party and my accessories. Minjee's party was themed vintage; so, it only made sense that everything was black and white. I had bought a sleeveless black velvet dress that stopped mid-thigh, it had a deep U-neck and a big white glittery belt. I also bought a white furry leopard printed jacket which I would wear up till my elbow. I made sure to pack my white pair of heeled boots with ragged edges that had just arrived along with a few accessories like a black and white handbag, a thick black chocker and big white diamond earrings along with a few rings and ear studs. Lastly, I kept a pair of pajamas handy just in case I felt like sleeping over at Minjee's place. Once I had packed everything, I took my bag, picked up my phone and headed downstairs and out of the house. Then I got into the car and told the driver to drop me to Minjee's place. On my way I called dad just to let him know that I was on my way to Minjee's house. When I reached, I got out of the car with my big suitcase like bag in one hand, not giving the driver the chance to carry it for me. I rang the bell with my empty hand and was greeted by Minjee's mom at the door she welcomed me and asked a maid to call Minjee down. As Minjee was coming down the stairs, I started singing the birthday song. Both of us started laughing and giggling at my silliness, by the time she reached the end of the stairs I was standing in front of her. Both of us hugged each other then I picked up my bag and let her mom know that we would be going to her room. Once we reached her room, we decided to just sit in each other's company talking and laughing about everything we were planning to do at the party. After a while we had to go to the party hall to see how the decorations look. Minjee was having her party in her parent's summer mansion. It was the perfect destination for her party, since almost everything in the house followed her vintage theme. Everything was high-end but gave a very 80's vibe. She had also planned an after party, a whole three days on her parents' yacht, it was something we were longing to do for a while but never really got the opportunity to do until now. It was just going to be me, Minjee and Suho. Suho is Minjee's cousin and all three of us are pretty good friends. But the after party wasn't until next week. We went to the party venue right after we stopped by at a donuts and milkshake place to have a little snack.The mansion was just as we had planned to set it up. The workers were still working on some last-minute details like the dim lights. Once we checked out the place we headed back to Minjee's house, where the stylist was waiting to do our hair, makeup and nails. In about two hours both of us were ready in our party clothes, shoes and all. I had a very different style of make-up on compared to what I usually go for but that didn't mean I wasn't in love with this style, it gave me a very unique look on my cheeks. All the pink making me look flushed, I had cat eyes and my lips were plump it was a very feminine look. My hair was straightened even more than I had done it in the morning, making it pencil straight leaving no curls behind. My bangs were set and sprayed in a way where it looked a little messy but complemented the flushed makeup. Minjee's look on the other hand was bold and fierce, she was wearing a black sequined strapless floor length dress, it was a backless dress with a big slit in the middle. Her accessories consisting of the big white diamond chocker that I just gifted her, a few layered chains, a few shiny rings dazzling her considerably long fingers, long shiny diamond earrings and her feet in pointed taupe heels with metal chains instead of a ribbon hanging around her ankle. She looked drop dead gorgeous, anyone who saw her would be able to tell she was the host of such an extravagant party. After our makeover we left the house and went to the mansion where the food was now ready and stalked on the long tables, we did come super early so we could stuff our faces before the guests arrive and judge us. So, we sat down and ate one of each type of dessert they had. Just as we finished, the guests started arriving. We had a lot of fun, we danced, did karaoke, ate a ton of cake, played truth or dare with our other friends and so much more all into the depths of the night. The party was over at around five in the morning and both of us were now back at Minjee's house. We decided that it would be best if I slept over at her house since it was already the next day. We were both completely drained and so we decided to just change out of our clothes and go to bed, I was so tired that I couldn't even search for my own pajamas so I just put on the first thing I found in Minjee's closet which was pretty normal between the two of us. We passed out on her bed as soon as our head hit the pillow.

We woke up in time for lunch. I had lunch with Minjee and her parents after which I packed all my things called my driver, said goodbye to her and left. Little did I know that once I reach home, I would be greeted with one of the biggest surprise of my life.

Chapter-2

THE ESCAPE

As soon as the car came to a halt I got out and walked to the door but when I opened the door, I heard loud screams and cries. I may be the daughter of a world-famous mafia but that doesn't mean I am used to hearing people scream. The noise was coming from under the house which meant something was happening in the basement, my bag fell from my hand as I ran down towards the stairs. Since I didn't have the patience to wait for the lift I walked into the basement and looked around hoping to find the source of the cries but I couldn't see anything until I walked deeper inside to the part where we had kept moms things, it was one of my favourite spots in the house, but to my dismay there was no one there either. Walking a little further I came across a room which probably just had some old junk I never wandered this deep into the basement so I didn't know but just as I stood in front of the door I heard the cries grow louder, my breathe hitched in my throat, my heart was pounding at an alarming rate. I was afraid to open the door but with my last ounce of courage I put my hand on the cold hard doorknob. My heart beating faster at every second that passed by, slowly twisting the knob and using the last of my strength to push the door open. I stopped in my tracks at the sight in front of me. It was dad standing there with two of his men by his side, but my heart forgot to breathe and my brain stopped functioning when I saw one of dad's bodyguard was beating up my maid, I didn't understand what was going on all I could do was yell asking them to stop. Once I screamed, everyone's attention was at me I was shocked, so I ran to dad and asked him what was going on. But before he could answer I saw my maid her whole body bruised up and bleeding, her clothes looked like she had got into a fight with a bear, scratches and purplish blue wounds covering her whole body most of which would scar. Just wondering for how long she would have to go through this for the wounds to show this badly, at this thought I burst into tears. Dad tried to calm me down, but it was useless until dad said something that made my whole-body freeze in shock. He said that my maid had killed mom, I was at a loss for words. When dad suddenly asked her why she had killed my mom, she didn't answer. So, dad's workers picked up the leather belt and started beating her continually. She beseeched over and over again until she let out a loud scream which was followed by something no one would have believed but somehow, I felt she was telling the truth. She said, "Ma'am had asked me to add the poison to the drink, I didn't know what it was for at the time; so, I obeyed my boss's orders" I asked dad what he was going to do to her but dad just told me that I didn't have to worry about that. Whatever dad was going to do wasn't going to be good I was sure she would be killed and her body never to be found again. So, I asked dad what if she was telling the truth, what if it was mom who did it to herself. Dad's face turned red with rage and before I could realise it, he had slapped me but as soon as he realized what he had done, he regretted it. My face was now red and my cheek was bleeding because the ring in his finger had cut my cheek, it was the wedding ring he never took off. Tears were streaming down my face as I stood there shocked while dad hugged me and tried to get me to calm down, but I couldn't take it anymore. I pushed him away and ran out of the room, through the large basement and into the elevator pushing on the button which was meant to close the doors, pushing hard and continuously taking all of my anger out on it, the door closed before dad could step in and stop me. Running out of the elevator and into my room as the doors of the elevator opened, locking the door behind me I sunk into the floor tears pooling in my eyes. Dad had followed by taking the stairs, but I had beaten him to my room and now he was outside my room banging the door asking to let him in. I just screamed, "Leave me alone" but he wouldn't budge he kept saying that he was sorry, and I knew he was. So I opened the door told him that I wanted to be alone he didn't say anything but after a few seconds he just nodded and left. I just shut my door and sat on my bed but just as I sat down my head started spinning. It felt as if someone was banging my head with a hammer. I didn't know what to do so I just lay on the bed closing my eyes trying to come to terms with all that happened today, feeling a heavy weight on my shoulders I drifted off to sleep.

Slowly peeling my eyes open after hearing something that sounded like a lion's roar only to realize it was my stomach. I was famished, I had forgotten to eat dinner after everything that had happened, I was so hungry that everything else around me didn't matter at this point. It was still around 12:00 at night so I thought I should just have a midnight snack. I then tiptoed my way to the kitchen; we had a little pancake batter left from breakfast so, I made myself some pancakes. I flipped over and plated the last of the pancakes, I took them upstairs to my room but as soon as I reached my room, I realized that I had forgotten the cutlery. So, without another thought I made my way back downstairs to get the cutlery. On my way back, I saw dad's room door was wide open and his study light was on. So I decided to see what he was doing I went inside and I saw dad asleep on his chair. I went towards him, I saw a few papers on his desk and I decided to take a look. But I couldn't believe my eyes there was a passport and a few documents. But on them there was a name that I recognized it belonged to Kim Aecha. The name was the same, but the picture was of my maids with another picture next to it, it was probably her childhood picture but it was the same picture of the little girl I saw the last time I fainted. I never put two and two together both that girl in my memory and my maid had the same name. I didn't understand, I mean Aecha was a very popular name. I needed to find out more, so I took pictures of all the documents I also took a picture of the passport. I went back to my room and picked up my laptop. Dad has a database of all the people in town it has all their important details and their picture, I opened the database and luckily dad's not good at keeping passwords. Once I got in, I searched for the name Kim Aecha, it took me some time but I found my maid's data, I clicked on her data and I read her family description but what shocked me was that it said she had an elder sister. Her name was Kim Bong-cha, so I searched for her and once I found her profile, I found out that she was dead. It said that she had died in an accident when she was 12. The details of her death were also given; it turns out she died when a truck crashed into her. I couldn't believe what I was reading could it mean that my maid was actually my sister, was I Kim Bong-cha before and reborn as Lee Nayeon. I had to be sure so I went to the basement to see if Aecha was still there. I saw her lying on the floor shivering because of the cold I was wearing a jacket so I took it off and put it on her cold body she was startled and backed away from me. I told her that I wouldn't hurt her but that wasn't really helping. So I got straight to the point I told her that I knew that I was her sister. She seemed shocked at first but she had finally loosened up a little, after a few minutes she finally spoke she said that she knew I would figure it out. I was still a little shocked, I knew by tomorrow she would be dead, I had to save her. Without thinking much, I decided that I would let her free and I would leave to my grandma's house which is in Busan until I could find out more. Busan was on the other side of the country so we had to leave right away. I untied her and took her with me to my room on the way I told her my plan. Then I took a few suitcases and packed all my important things then I asked Aecha if she had anything important in her room that she wanted to take with her. She said that she did, so we had to go to her room. Once we reached her room she quickly went to her wardrobe and pulled out a wooden box with a pretty flower emblem on it. I was understandably curious so I asked her what was inside, "It's a surprise I'll show you when the time is right" she said. She then took out a bag and put the few pairs of clothes she had in it. Then we headed to the living room where all the credit cards and all the money was kept. I picked up my credit cards and the car keys. Then we headed out of the door to the garage where the cars are kept at night. We got into the car and luckily, I knew how to drive but I wasn't legally old enough to drive but I didn't have any other choice. "Unnie why don't you put your bag in the back" I asked, she was slightly astounded when I called her unnie (unnie is the Korean word for older sister generally used by younger females), "are you uncomfortable with me calling you unnie" she shook her head still in shock and probably in pain from all the wounds in her neck and face. But I could tell she found it vaguely strange since, she used to call me unnie when she was younger. I just smiled at her trying to understand everything from her point of view, that's when I realized we had to get going. So, I put the keys in the engine, the car roaring to a start, pressing the pedal softly the car budged forward. When we had reached halfway to the airport, I realized that we hadn't booked a flight so I asked Aecha unnie if she could book a flight for both of us and she could use my credit card to pay. But she said she didn't have a phone, I wondered how she could live without a phone, I just handed her my phone and told her how to book the flight. After almost half an hour of driving, I got a call from dad but I just switched my phone off trying to focus on the road ahead of me. The rest of the ride to the airport was quiet. Once we had reached, I parked the car and both of us took the luggage out we then walked inside the airport and finished our baggage check and our security check. We had quite some time before we had to board our flight. So, we decided to check out the duty free. And I saw a Phone showroom so I decided it would be the best time to buy Aecha unnie a phone, so we went inside, and I got her the latest phone. Once we had bought the phone, I helped unnie get it running. I also got both of us headphones because I had left mine at home. Then I plugged in my headphones and started playing songs from the playlist I had created as songs continued to play suddenly the song that mom, dad and I loved, started playing we used to dance to this song together all the time. Suddenly I couldn't believe what I was doing I was running away from home; I was running away from my dad the person who I love most in this world. I couldn't hold my tears I started sobbing quietly, unnie understood something was wrong she hugged me and said that she was very sorry that I had to go through all this because of her. First the death of my mother, then leaving my dad and running away from home. She also said that it was alright if I wanted to go back home that I could go, and she would find somewhere to live. But I couldn't leave her, she was my sister it didn't matter if she was my sister in this life or my last life. And I knew that I wasn't running away from home I was just clearing my head before I could go back and explain everything to dad. I had calmed down a little by this time when suddenly unnie said that it was time to show me the surprise. So, she opened her bag and took out the wooden box and handed it to me saying that mom would have wanted me to have it. I took it happily because I didn't really remember my mom from my past life, I opened it and inside was a small circular pendant two intertwined flowers imprinted on it. I really liked it so I asked if it was for me. I was pleased when unnie said that it was for me, I put it on with a big smile on my face. Just as I put it on the announcement for our gate came, the gates had opened so we could start boarding. Both of us got in the flight and sat in our seats which were luckily next to each other. It was going to be a long flight, so I had brought a few magazines so, that both of us didn't get bored. We didn't speak that much the whole ride because both of us hadn't slept well so we slept for most of the time. When we reached, we got our luggage from the conveyer belts and headed outside, then we took a taxi to go to grandma's house on the way there I explained to unnie about my relationship with grandma. Only after mom passed away did she find out about dad's work, just as I said the last word, I realized that she didn't know about dad's work. But I think my face clearly showed that I was worried as she said that I didn't have to worry as mom had told her about dad being a mafia. I was relieved that I didn't have to lie, then continued and told her that as soon as grandma found out she cut ties with dad but still kept in touch with me. Soon we had reached grandma's house. Both of us got out and the driver helped us to take our luggage out. We went to the front door and rang the bell.

Chapter-3

GRANDMA'S SURPRISE

Grandma opened the door and she was visibly animated, which was understandable after all I was seeing her after 3 whole years. Once we greeted each other we went inside and grandma asked how I decided to come over so suddenly not that she was complaining. So, I said, "The thing is I came here without telling dad, I'll explain everything but for now this is Aecha unnie do you mind if she stays here" grandma was confused but said, "As long as you tell me everything." I sat down on the couch, grandma next to me and unnie awkwardly standing there. Grandma ushered unnie to sit down so she took a seat opposite the both of us. And we sat there until I explained everything that had happened yesterday, by the end of the conversation grandma was aghast. Not knowing what to say she stood up and took a good look at unnie, "I do see a resemblance between the two of you and it is likely that you have a sibling from your past life since you don't have any siblings now" she said still staring at unnie contently "but Nay he is your father and your parents must come before anything else so I want you to talk to him, take your time but make sure you do it" she said sternly, nodding I asked where me and unnie would stay. Grandma took us upstairs where all the rooms were, which is also where my old room was it was still the same. It had my bright pink bed and fairy lights with my photos stuck on it. Then there was my cupboard filled with my clean and nicely folded clothes, my favourite purple curtains covering the windows and a large balcony filled with beautiful potted plants and flowers and not to forget the big TV. I used to love playing in grandma's house as kid because her house has a lot of balconies and all of them connect to each other; me and grandma would play endless games of tag and hide-and-seek. The walls of my room had a few of the pictures I had drawn as a kid framed and hung on them, the inside of cupboard was filled with a few more recent sketches that were stuck on the door. But none of the clothes that were in the cupboard would fit me. I then asked grandma where unnie would be sleeping she said that unnie could sleep in the extra room. There was a nice plain white bed with a green floral bed cover along with a similar type of pillows, there were a few paintings here and there on the walls, there were white curtains that covered the huge window, a big cupboard and a TV. Grandma told, me and unnie to go and freshen up and she would get lunch ready. So, both of us went to our rooms and I took a shower, then changed into a pretty white button up off shoulder dress with frills for sleeves. I then brushed through my hair leaving it open. Once I was ready, I went down where I saw grandma and unnie waiting for me downstairs. Me and unnie set the table together while grandma finished cooking the food, it looked delicious. I went and sat down next to grandma while unnie sat opposite to me. We all finished the food really quickly and thanked grandma for the food. I really wanted to go out and see how much had changed in the past three years. So, we all went for a drive. Grandma drove us around the city, we were back in about two hours. On the way back I realized that I hadn't told Minjee about this, I couldn't tell her everything anyway so I just messaged her saying that I would be away for some time. After we reached home grandma realized that unnie's cuts had to be cleaned or they could get infected so she brought her first aid kit and handed it to me. She then made unnie sit on the couch, I opened the first aid kit and pulled out an ointment and a big chunk of cotton, I tore out a lump of cotton from it and handed it to grandma who applied the ointment on it and started cleaning unnie's wounds following in her footsteps I applied some of the ointment on the cotton ball cleaned unnie's painful wounds and cuts. It broke my heart to see her whimper in pain every time the cool liquid on the cotton touched her burning wounds. It was a gut-wrenching sight, but it had to be done to stop her from suffering any further. After all of unnie's wounds were cleaned and bandaged grandma proposed we play a few board games to distract unnie from the pain. So, we all sat around the coffee table in the living room and played multiple board games until it was dinner time. After dinner we all just sat around the fire place in the backyard and spoke about everything from unnie's parents to some old memories me and grandma held dearly. Soon I was tired so I excused myself and went to my room, we were probably going to be out all day tomorrow because unnie doesn't have any clothes since we didn't really think of packing clothes in that rush of last night. I haven't been able to sleep properly these past few days and I needed my sleep. So, I changed into a comfy pair of pajamas and just lay on my bed until I was asleep.

I woke up the next morning with the sound of pots and pans being banged. I laughed to myself because this was something mom used to do to wake me up. And now, I knew where she learned it from. I got up and went to the bathroom, brushed my teeth and washed my face. After I was done, I went downstairs and saw grandma getting the breakfast ready; she was making pancakes which reminded me of the night I ran away from home if it wasn't for my hunger, I wouldn't be here.

Once I was out of my thoughts I went and helped grandma in the kitchen while unnie came down and set the table. Once the pancakes were ready, I put them all in a plate and put chocolate syrup on it along with a few berries and then served grandma, unnie and myself. After we were done, I went upstairs to take out all my clothes from my suitcase and arrange it in my cupboard because it was getting difficult for me to find my clothes in that big suitcase. As soon as I was done, I went and took shower after which I changed into a white crop top, green cargo pants and a leather jacket, I also took a black bag and put my phone and other important things in it. I was now ready to go shopping, I went down and waited for unnie and grandma. Soon grandma was also done but there was no sign of unnie. So, I went to check up on her. I knocked on her door and she opened but she was only wearing a bathrobe I asked her why she was not wearing any clothes and she said that she didn't have anything to wear so I took her to my room and told her that she could pick out anything she liked from my closet since we were practically sisters. And with that I left the room so she could change, she came down wearing my blue floral dress with her hair braided. The car ride to the mall was rather quiet but when we reached the mall both me and unnie got down and grandma went to park the car. We went to many different stores and bought several things I was using my credit card to pay even though grandma insisted on paying I didn't want her to burden herself because of us and anyway I hadn't used much of my allowance for the past few months so I was loaded. Once we got tired shopping and had enough pairs of clothes to last 2 months, we decided to eat something but this time grandma paid, each of us had a burger, a packet of fries and a can of soda. After that we all decided it was time to go back home. So, we took all our bags and put it in the trunk of the car, we all sat inside and started back home. In all of our excitement and chatter about new clothes, neither me or unnie realized we were already back home. All of us got out of the car we had all picked up a few bags, I walked towards the door to unlock it so, it would be easy for the others to come in. But when I went closer to the door, I saw dad sitting there I didn't understand how he found out I was here no one else knew other than Aecha unnie, grandma and me. But it couldn't be any of them, I didn't know what had gotten in to me because I just passed by him without saying a word or even acknowledging his presence, I opened the door, my back facing him. But before I could get in dad called for me, he said, "Ignore me all you want Nay but in the end of the day I am and always will be your father, but I won't understand what went wrong if you don't talk to me." That was when the strong front I was putting up finally broke, tears streamed down my face wetting my cheeks, I turned on my heel and ran into dad's arms hugging him so tightly that I felt like he would disappear if I let go. He hugged me back cupping my face in his palms and wiping every tear my eyes shed. We just stood there the only sound were my quiet sobs, grandma broke the silence ushering all of us inside. We all got in and I closed the door behind me we all walked into the living room and took our places on the couch; we had been standing outside for quite a while which led me to catch a slight cold so I got up and asked if anyone wanted any coffee, I knew it was going to be a long night and I deserved a coffee. I made everyone coffee, placed the cups onto a tray and walked back into the living room where everyone was dead silent. It was a little eerie but I knew there was no going back, I handed everyone their coffee and sat down next to dad, grandma and unnie sitting on the other side of the room. No one said a word which made sense since dad and grandma aren't on speaking terms ever since mom's death and unnie was a whole other picture. This time I had to break the silence by asking dad how he knew where I was. Turns out when he realized I wasn't home he contacted Minjee. But as he learned I wasn't there he started to get worried, he thought of where else I could be, coming to the conclusion that the only other place I could go to was grandma's. But just to be sure he checked my passport status, credit cards and a lot of other things until he found that I bought two tickets to Busan and he booked the next flight here. Then dad asked me why I had run away. So, I explained the whole story to him, he told me that he didn't fully believe the 'rebirth thing' as he liked to call it but was alright with the fact that I cared for unnie as a sister and back. After that was said dad asked me when I was planning to come back home, I told him that I would come back as soon things would become alright between him and grandma. He was very confused. He didn't think I would say that, but he said that he didn't mind. I looked at grandma and asked her if she would want to fix the broken bond between them. She said,"I knew about your father's work a few months before your mother's death itself, at that time I didn't know what do but after my daughter left this world, I decided that I didn't want to be related to anyone who got paid to murder innocent people. But I didn't want to lose you Nay, and if it would make you smile then I think its best we let go of whatever happened in the past and move towards the future." With an outspread smile I looked over to the person who hadn't spoken this whole time, Aecha unnie. I asked her what she wanted to do now that everything is settled. But before I could finish my sentence dad interrupted me telling her that if she wants, she could come back home with us and live a normal life. I asked dad if he was really alright with unnie coming back, he said that it wasn't unnie's fault mom passed away and he would explain what actually happened to mom later. So, I asked unnie what she wanted to do she said that if grandma was alright with it, she would like to stay with grandma for a few weeks until she is ready to come and live with me in Seoul. Thankfully grandma was more than happy to let unnie stay with her. By this time, we were all tired so we decided to go to bed. Grandma slept in her room, me and dad shared the guest room which unnie was using before, while unnie slept in my room.

The next day me and dad sat and booked the flight ticket for both of us to go back to Seoul. We were going back in three days, dad wanted to go back tomorrow but I wanted to spend some more time with grandma. So, dad said that if I agreed to go back in three days, he would book tickets for grandma to come to Seoul next week and so I agreed.

Before I knew it, three days had passed and it was time to go back, all my things were packed and in the cab's trunk. I was now saying goodbye to my teary-eyed grandma. Her tears showed how much she missed me these past years. Dad tried to console her by reminding her that she would be seeing me next month, once she had calmed, we let her know that we would be leaving. We were getting late for our flight so I said my goodbyes to both grandma and unnie. The ride to the airport was quiet, we spent most of the time in the airport and flight reading magazines and listening to music or arguing over which song was better. Once we reached home, I ran to my room and jumped on my bed. I missed home, it's wasn't like I didn't like grandma's house, but it's always best when you're in your own house.

Weeks had passed in a heartbeat. Grandma and unnie had come and gone and it had been a few days since unnie moved back to Seoul. She was staying with me and dad. I got the courage to start going back to school again and unnie went to college. We would meet up after our classes, sometimes with unnie's friends and sometimes without. Everything was going well and I thought I would be able to live peacefully but I couldn't have been more wrong. I was losing someone very important to me.

THE END

PART-2

Chapter-4

BACK TO NORMAL

Things were going well. I had made a few friends at school but I was losing my best friend, Minjee wouldn't tell me what was wrong, all she said that she was mad that I wouldn't tell her where I had gone. It's not that that I don't trust her I'm just worried she'd think I was going crazy. So, I thought I would just give her some space until she forgets about it. Weeks passed and Minjee still hadn't spoken to me she was always with Suho and Jimin. Jimin is a year younger to us. And I guess she's now Minjee's best friend, I was gone for a week and Minjee already found a replacement for me. I couldn't believe she had the audacity to ignore me for so long, I couldn't take it anymore so I decided that I was going to throw my entire ego out of the door and speak to her today. 'The whole day flew by and I still haven't spoken to her' I thought as I walked out of my last class for the day and to the main gate where I usually wait for unnie to pick me up. As I was waiting, I saw Minjee walking by with Jimin and Suho I knew that this was my chance I walked up to her, stopping right behind her before calling out her name. She turned to face me, when she saw me, her eyes widened, "What do you want" she asked. "I don't know what I did wrong but, I'm sorry, please accept my apology" I replied hoping she would accept my apology. But it did the total opposite. My thoughtless apology seemed to have gotten her even more mad. With a red face she yelled back getting the attention of everyone else, "You're the worst friend anyone could ever have, firstly you ran away without a trace and then also decided not to attend my after party that we had planned with so much effort and finally you give me such a baseless apology." That's when I realized that this was about the after party, I felt really sorry but I didn't know how to explain it to her so I just stood there starring at my shoes like an idiot, only to look up when I heard her scoff and walk away with Jimin and Suho. After they had left, I started to walk back home I couldn't wait for unnie anymore I just wanted to get back home away from all the people who were glaring at me and murmuring to themselves. I knew this feeling very well this had happened before when mom passed away but Minjee was there with me, she held my hand and walked through the gate with me. Head held up high she didn't let go of my hand even after we had reached home. She cared so much for me and I lied to her and blew her off on the day we had planned for since we were little. I really had to explain to her that I was sorry but, how could I? Just pondering about everything I had reached home. It was only a 10–15-minute walk from home to school. Immediately after I got inside, I rushed to my bedroom, threw my bag on the single seater sofa chair and threw myself on my bed only to repeatedly hit my head on the wall to try and come think of a way to make it up to Minjee and give her a proper explanation. After a few minutes of banging my hand, I was left with a throbbing headache and realization, that the only way was to try and give her an explanation of what happened with hope that she'll forgive me and maybe also a small apology present which I may or may not use to bribe her to forgiving me. And that's why I was now searching online for a good gift for her. Just as I was doing that, I got a call it was from unnie then I remembered that I hadn't told her that I was walking home, quickly I clicked on the answer button only to get shouted at, "I was worried sick when I didn't see you at the gate and I wasn't able to reach you, so I called Minjee, who told me what happened and that she hadn't seen you after, do you know how many horrifying scenarios on what happened to you went on in my head at that." I told her that I had walked home as I didn't want to stay there. Unnie seemed pretty worried and mad so, she just hung up on me with a deep sigh. She was home in the next few minutes. She was still mad as she came up to my room and asked me why I had not waited for her I told her that everyone was staring at me and whispering about me and I couldn't stand there and hear them talk nonsense about me. Unnie had understood that I felt hurt and lonely, so she apologised for yelling at me, but I had understood that she was genuinely worried about me just how an elder sister would have been. I then told her that I was planning to call Minjee over tomorrow so we could sort things out and I also told her about the gift I was planning on giving her and that I needed help in deciding what to get her. We both then sat together and decide that we should get matching diamond bracelets for both me and Minjee. Now all I had to do was wait for dad to come home so I could show it to him and ask him what he thinks. And so, I decided to finish my homework and prepare for the test I had tomorrow until dad came. I had a test in algebra and I totally hate math but it's not like I have a choice this is the problem with school, unlike home-school you can't make up excuses to get out of tests. Once I finished my homework and was done preparing for the test I went downstairs and sat down next to unnie who was watching TV as she didn't have anything else to do today. Both of us watched a few reality-tv-shows until dad came home. As soon as dad was home all three of us went to the dining room where we had dinner, in 15 minutes we were finished with dinner and back in the living room. We all usually sit together and talk right after dinner, today we were talking about how popular unnie has become in college and also how many friends she has, that's when I remembered about Minjee. So I told dad what had happened in school and how I was planning to call Minjee home and not to forget the bracelet. He said that I should go ahead and get the bracelet and that it was a good idea to speak things out with Minjee. So, I went back to my room to order the bracelet, I hit the order button and I felt sleep wash over me, my body was drained after everything that had happened today so I switched off my laptop went downstairs to tell unnie and dad goodnight before heading to bed.

The next morning, surprisingly I woke up on my own. It was around 7:00AM when I woke up, I had an hour before I had to head to school. So, I got out of bed and made my way to the bathroom where I took a shower and got dressed then I headed downstairs to get some breakfast. Me, dad and unnie had breakfast together after which dad left to work. Unnie and I headed back to our rooms to pack our things before leaving for school and college. I took my bag and put in my phone, my laptop and the 8-page essay I had typed down and printed out for my English class. I also kept some cash for lunch and for the cab ride to the jewellery shop and back, I have to go and pick up the bracelets myself since I they don't have delivery options for today. Once I had finished packing, I went to unnie's room to check if she was ready, just as I knocked on her door, she pulled it open, a sling bag hanging on her bare shoulder, she was wearing a shoulder less blue top with black high waist jeans. Soon both of us walked out of the house and into unnie's car. Yes, dad bought unnie a car I still don't know how dad was suddenly alright with unnie's presence, I have tried asking him but he always tells me that he will tell me when the time is right. On the way to school, I called grandma, me and unnie took turns talking to her turns out grandma is planning to come to Seoul soon. Both me and unnie got really excited, unnie had somehow became a part of our family now. But we couldn't continue our conversation since we were now right in front of the school's main gate so both of us said goodbyes, I hung up, put my phone inside, said goodbye to unnie and got out of the car. That's when I realized that my classes don't start till 8:30 and it was just 8:05AM. I used to come early so me and Minjee could spend some time together before class because we have only two classes together. And both of them were on Thursday. I guess it's that miserable part of the day again where I get to be all lonely not that I don't feel miserably lonely all day anyway but things were going to change from tomorrow, everything was going back to normal. I didn't really have anything to do until I remembered that I still hadn't checked with Minjee if she could come over tomorrow. So, while heading to class I took my phone out from the bag and messaged Minjee I started with a "hi". She replied to me within a few minutes, I was glad she replied; I low-key expected her to ignore me. I then got straight to the point and asked her if she was free tomorrow, she said that she was so, I told her that there was something I wanted to discuss with her. I asked her if she could come over tomorrow. She said that she could, I didn't know what else to say so I just ended the conversation with a smiley emoji. This means that she was coming tomorrow I was now really excited but I was sucked out of this excitement and pulled back to reality when I heard the bell ring, I rushed to my first class without a second thought. The whole school day went by without anything new. And now I was sitting in the park next to my school waiting for the cab to arrive. Soon the cab had arrived and I was heading to the jewellery shop, the shop wasn't very far away I was back home in about an hour. As soon as I got home, I went to unnie's room and showed her what I had got. Each bracelet had 2 circles with each of our names engraved on it. Unnie really liked it she said that I was the type of friend everyone would want. She even liked the box it came in, it was a circular box in pink colour and it had a velvet cloth wrapped on top with a golden bow. I couldn't wait till tomorrow things were finally going to go back to normal. Dad had come home early so after I was finished with all my school work, we all ate dinner and went to bed.

Chapter-5

THE ARRIVAL

The next morning, I woke up, got ready and headed to school. The day went by, all my classes were over and now I was back home and waiting. It was finally time for Minjee to arrive. Just as I was making sure everything was ready the doorbell rang that meant Minjee was here, I went and opened the door. We both then greeted each other and got inside. I asked Minjee to sit and then went to the kitchen to ask my new maid to get us something to eat. Since the time we came back from grandma's house we have hired this maid to take unnie's place. Once I had told my maid I headed back to the living room and sat next to Minjee. Just as I sat, I started to speak, "I called you home because I wanted to make things clear and that I don't want to fight anymore, why exactly aren't you talking to me" I asked. She said that she was mad that I had ditched her on the day of her 'after party' and I didn't have a proper reason for not coming there. All I had done was sent her a message saying that I was out of town. So, I then told her that I was at grandma's house, she went on to ask me why I had gone there I replied saying, "It's a long story". "I'm free all day" she said an irritated look on her face I had to say something but I couldn't tell her everything so I just told her that my dad had found out who had who had poisoned mom she was our maid but I had a strong feeling that it wasn't her, she claimed that she had not done it and dad was planning to report her but that night I had found out that she was my sister but from my last life so I ran away with her to my grandma's house but dad found us and brought us back. This was probably a lot to take in for her, she didn't say anything. So I said, it didn't make sense at all even to me I left my dad behind because of something my maid or now my sister had said. But I couldn't lose Minjee because of this "It's ok if you don't believe me but I don't want any of this to affect our friendship" I said hoping she'd understand. At this she answered, "I trust you but I can't understand how you found out your maid is your sister from your last life" she seemed sceptical. And so, I told her that I had flashbacks which showed me my old family and everything else. She seemed to have believed me, that's when I realized that I had to give her the bracelet, I told her that I was really sorry that I had missed her 'after party' and I knew that this might not make up for it but I still wanted to give it to her. So I took out the box and gave it to her she was surprised and excited she opened it quickly and took out the bracelet she looked really happy she said that she loved it and quickly put it on. I told her that I was glad she liked it and then I took out mine showing her that I got myself a matching one, even I put mine one. Right after putting it on both of us went up to my room and we spoke about what all had happened in the past few weeks. Then Minjee asked where Aecha unnie was so I told her that she was in her cram school. Soon Minjee had left, unnie and dad were back home and we were all watching T.V. and talking as we had already finished dinner, I had just finished telling dad and unnie how well things went between me and Minjee. When dad said that he wouldn't be home for two days as he had to go to Daegu. I was fine with it because I was used to dad being away, even unnie didn't seem to mind. Anyway, I had asked Minjee to come over tomorrow. After discussing this dad asked if we were planning to stay up all night and watch a few movies as tomorrow was a Saturday and none of us had school. I wanted to watch movies and so did unnie so, we decided that we would watch movies in our home theatre. Once that was decided me and unnie told goodnight to dad who was making his way up the stairs to go to bed, he wanted to join us but he had an early flight tomorrow. First, we went to the kitchen to pick out a few different types of snacks to eat during the movie after that was done, I asked the maid to bring it to the home theatre and then me and unnie made our way upstairs to go and get our pillows and blankets from our rooms so we could be more comfortable. After that was done, we went to the home theatre and picked out a movie once we decided on the movie, we sat on the sofa chairs as the movie began to play. Soon even the snacks were brought and as time flew two movies were already done both me and unnie fell asleep during the third movie, in the theatre itself.

The next morning both me and unnie were woken up by dad, he woke us up as he had to leave for the airport. So, we went downstairs with him where he took his luggage and made his way to the door, I hugged dad and then me and unnie told him goodbye. Once dad had left, I went back to my room where I took a shower and got dressed, I planned to spend today chilling at home with unnie unless she had other plans. I put on a black full sleeved T-shirt with a white strapped dress on top. After I was ready, I went to unnie's room but she was still in the bathroom so I went downstairs to wait for her at the breakfast table. Almost half an hour later she came down I was very curious on why she had taken so long so I asked. She said that it was because she was going to meet her parents, I got really excited at that as whenever I asked unnie about how they are and if I could meet them, she would always ignore the topic with a, "maybe next time." But it's the first time she let me know before she went to meet them so understandably, I asked her if I could come along at first, she was a little confused but after some thinking she decided that they should probably come home. I thought it was a great idea, I really wanted to meet them. So, I told unnie to invite them right away and I went and told our maid to make a very fancy dinner, I then quickly finished my breakfast and went upstairs to decide what I was going to wear. After trying on almost a dozen outfits I found an outfit which was perfect, it contained a black sleeveless leather dress I bought when I was shopping for Minjee's birthday along with a furry white coat, fish net stockings and white dazzling boots. I went crazy while picking out accessories, picking a metal chain choker with a few necklaces of different sizes to layer and finally grabbing a handful of woven bracelets. It was the middle of summer outside but cool as the winter breeze inside, hence I could wear whatever I wanted at home. Once I picked my outfit, I went to unnie's room to see what she was planning on wearing and because I wanted to let her know that the maid wanted us to come down when we are free to pick out a menu for dinner. As I was making my way to her room, I had this feeling that I was forgetting something but I just brushed it off as I was now in front of unnie's room, as I entered her room, I saw her wearing a black dressshirt and her hair curled giving her a smoky look, her makeup complimenting her eyes, making her jaw look sharp and making her lips plump I couldn't help but compliment her. I think she hadn't noticed me before as she looked in my direction confused as soon as she saw me standing at her door, she smiled looking at me and called me in. I walked inside and she asked me to sit down, I sat on her bed and told her that we had to go down to decide the menu. She then told me that she had to talk to me once we had decided the menu,

I didn't know what she wanted to tell me but I agreed. We then went downstairs to the kitchen where the maid was waiting for us, we quickly chose a few of our favourite courses and asked the maid to serve us lunch. Both of us finished our lunch quickly without talking much time. Once we were done, we walked to my room where we sat down on thesofa and I asked unnie what she wanted to talk to me about she said, "I'm not sure if I want to let mom and dad know that uncle Lee is the leader of a gang of mafias." Confused I replied, "It's alright if you don't want to let them know about dad being a mafia but I don't see the need for you to lie." Looking at her I could tell what I said made her a little angry so I told her that she is right her parents might get frightened if they found out she was living with a mafia. I think she understood my concern as she told me that the only reason, she didn't want to tell them is because they might separate us out of fear of something happening to her. I realized that she was right so I agreed to make sure that they don't find out about dad's actual work. After I agreed to it unnie let me know that they would be there in about 2 hours so I had a lot of time till I had to get ready. As unnie was leaving the room I took my phone to check my messages as I hadn't used it since morning that's when I saw Minjee's message, she said she was on her way but the thing was that she had sent that message almost 45 mins before I got worried Minjee's house is only 20 mins away and she still hadn't reached. I called her but she wasn't answering so I messaged her asking her where she was, she replied in about one and a half hour saying that she wouldn't be able to make it. This wasn't like her she would usually be very apologetic if she has to cancel on me. I felt something was wrong but before I could think of anything else unnie barged into my room asking me why I am not ready yet, she told me that her parents messaged her saying that they had already started. And I hadn't even started getting ready so I told unnie that I would get ready quickly and that she didn't have to worry.

Chapter-6

UNNIE'S PARENTS

With that said unnie left my room, I quickly changed into the outfit I had picked out earlier and almost half an hour later I was fully ready my make up on point, I had heavy mascara on and had gone for a more cat eye like look today, my naturally pouty lips shining because of the glittery lip gloss I had applied. My hair held into a loose French braid with a few baby hairs and front hair pulled out to look a little messy. I was now ready to head downstairs. With excitement I got out of my room and stood in front of the stair--case holding the railing with shaky hands, just as I took my first step down the stairs the doorbell rang. Letting me know that they were finally here, I hurried down the stairs almost tripping over twice. Unnie was already standing near the door waiting for me, sprinting to the door and stopping beside unnie just before the maid opened the door. And there stood unnie's parents who were also my previous parents if that made any sense. I smiled at them and bowed continuously as unnie greeted them (bowing is a way to show respect to elders of someone you look upto; the deeper you bow the more respect you show). Then unnie introduced me to them as Nayeon at this moment I wondered if they knew that I was their daughter. So, as they sat on the couch, I told them that I have to check on something and that I would be back soon, unnie seemed confused so I walked up to her and whispered to her asking her to join me in the back yard. She then said, "Mom, dad I'll be back" and followed me to the back of the house where she asked me what had happened. I then asked her if her parents knew that I was their daughter before. She thought for a moment and said, "They know that you were their daughter." After that was out of the way me and unnie headed back to the living room where her parents or should I say Mr and Mrs Kim were waiting. When we reached the living room both of them were in the middle of a conversation and as soon as they saw me and unnie they stopped talking, Mr Kim asked me if we could take a tour of our house as they had never been to a mansion before. I agreed as we had some time to spare before dinner and I thought it would awkward if we just sit there, after all I'm meeting them for the first time and I don't really know them. So, me and unnie gave her parents a tour of our house and as I said before our house is really big so it took about 45 minutes to cover the inside of our house after that we went to the backyard and just sat by the pool for a while. But soon our maid came out to let us know that dinner is ready so we went back inside to the dining room where I sat next to Mrs Kim next to whom unnie and her dad were sitting. The maid served the food and we spoke about many different things like how our school was going and about where dad was and how his work was going but never once did, we talk about Kim Bong-cha and I didn't want to bring that up as it could be a sensitive topic for them. Turns out unnie's parents really liked our backyard so after dinner we all went back there and sat on the campfire, I had lit up the fire so we decided to have our dessert in the backyard itself. I then asked our maid to bring us our desert outside, she brought out the ice cream and handed it out to each one of us, before we knew it all our bowls were empty. After dessert unnie's parents had left and it was just the two of us again. I was tired so I told unnie that I would be going to bed and headed to my room. As soon as I got to my room, I jumped on my bed I was feeling very tired, I just wanted to sleep so I lay on my bed and then I remembered that I hadn't called dad. So, I called him he must have been at his hotel room as he answered the call almost immediately, I told him about how unnie's parents had come over he wasn't very happy that I hadn't asked him before. So, I apologised and promised him that I would ask him next time, soon dad said that he was tired and that he would call me later. Now I was really tired but I knew I wouldn't be able to sleep with these clothes so I changed out of them quickly before crawling back into bed and pulling the covers on myself. Within no time I had slipped into dreamland.

The next day, I woke up on my own as I didn't have school. I really didn't want to get out of bed, I just felt like something was bugging me today. I didn't know what it was, it just felt like something was wrong. Even though I really don't want to, I drag myself out of bed and head to the bathroom to freshen up and try to get rid of whatever is bothering me. After I took a shower, I change into a grey oversized shirt with ripped jeans, I usually don't wear oversized clothes but today was an exception since it felt like a warm hug which I felt like I needed. I then tied my hair into a messy bun and went downstairs to the living room where unnie was sitting and going through her phone I asked her if she had already finished breakfast and she said she had just eaten an apple as she was dieting. So, I made my way to dining room where the maid was setting up the table for me, I sat down and started to eat by the time I was done, unnie was sitting next to me in the dining room and having her second apple. The maid then took my plate and cutlery and made her way to the kitchen where she had to wash the dishes. Unnie was still immersed in her phone so I asked her if she had anything to do today, she said she didn't but she felt like having some Chinese food. I wondered what had happened to her diet but I didn't want to say anything so I told her we could ask our cook to make something for us. I then headed to the kitchen where our cook was putting on some lip gloss, I asked her if she was going somewhere. She told me it was her grandson's first birthday today and her son-in-law and daughter were throwing a big party. She said that she had already informed dad a month ago. I told her that he hadn't told me anything about it, dad must have forgotten, he is getting old. So, I told her that she can go and enjoy in her grandson's party, me and unnie would just order something or we would go out to eat. After letting her know that she could leave I went back to the dining room where unnie was, I then told her that our cook was taking a leave today so we had to order Chinese food instead. Unnie suggested that we should go and get the food ourselves so we get a reason to get out of the house. I thought it was a good idea and, in that way, we could get some donuts too. Unnie asked me if it would be alright if we got food right away since she had other things to do later, I didn't mind so I said yes, unnie said that she had to get dressed and so she asked me to wait for her as I was already dressed. As unnie went to her room I went to mine to get my bag. As I got to my room, I kept my wallet in my bag with my phone and went back downstairs to wait for unnie. Unnie took almost half an hour to get ready even though we were just going to get lunch. She came down wearing a blue top with a black skirt and she was also carrying her purse. We were now ready to leave, unnie grabbed the car keys from the rack and we headed to the car, she drove us to the restaurant, we ordered our food through the drive through. After we had gotten our lunch, we went to get donuts.

Chapter-7

MINJEE

We reached the donut shop, me and unnie got out of the car and went inside, we decided to get a dozen of donuts so we could eat some after dinner and maybe save some for dad too as he was coming back tomorrow morning. I waited at a table for unnie while she ordered but then I spotted Minjee she was with Suho and she was crying, I wanted to know what was going on so I went closer to them to try to understand what was going on. I know it was wrong to eavesdrop on them but something was wrong and for some reason Minjee hadn't told me anything. But when I went near them, I heard Minjee saying "I can't believe her dad is a mafia, I am afraid to talk to her now what should I do?" I couldn't believe it she had found out, I couldn't even hear Suho's response as my eyes were filled with tears threatening to fall from my eyes, I was in shock my face had turned pale I didn't know what to do anymore. I looked over to unnie who was taking the box of donuts from the cashier. She looked over in my direction as I ran out of the shop to the car and stood in front of the car as streams of tears flowed faster than my heartbeat, I wasn't able to control myself even though people were staring at me and unnie came running towards me with the donuts still in her hand. As she came closer to me, I begged her to unlock the car, she unlocked the car and, in an instant, I was inside still sobbing uncontrollably. Unnie got in the car, put the donuts down and asked me what was wrong; I told her that I had overheard Minjee's conversation with Suho. She told me that this was bound to happen and that Minjee was anyway going to find out someday and it was better she found out now than later. She also told me that there was nothing I could do but try to talk to her and explain my situation. I knew unnie was right, I had to find a way to tell Minjee my situation. After I had calmed down, I asked unnie if we could go back home, unnie started driving. The ride home was quiet, neither of us uttered a word. Only when we reached home did we speak, unnie asked me if I would be having lunch in my room, I did want to be alone so I can think of what to say to Minjee so I said yes. Unnie then took out my lunch from the take away cover and handed it to me I took it and went upstairs to my room where I kept my food on my table and got on my bed. I sat on my bed and took out my phone from my bag, unlocked my phone and tried calling Minjee but she wasn't answering. So, I just texted her, I wanted to make sure I tell her everything so I said "Dear Minjee, I know that you might be very confused, mad and a lot of other things but I want to let you know that I never meant to hide any of this from you, I was just scared that you would get scared of me and keep your distance from me. I am sorry I lied to you all these years it's just that I had no friends ever since I was a little girl. And that day in school when a girl had pushed me in hallways you were the only one who walked up to me and asked me if I was alright and at that moment, I knew I had to treasure you and make sure nothing breaks us apart. I know I might sound like a weirdo but I never for a second regretted being your friend and I hope you feel the same way. I knew it was wrong of me of not telling you the truth even after all that you did for me. You embarrassed yourself just to get a smile out of me, you ruined your reputation in front of the whole school by doing weird things to see me happy. And even after all that I lied to you only because I didn't want to be lonely, but let me tell u something I never meant to hurt you, and if you plan on forgiving me, I promise I will never lie to you ever again. I am sorry for everything, I was really selfish and I hope you forgive me. Yours, Nayeon." As I wrote each word tears streamed down my cheeks. I meant every word I said, I hesitated but after a lot of thinking and crying I finally clicked send. I felt like a weight had been lifted of my shoulder, and that's when unnie knocked on my door. I rushed to the mirror and saw my eyes all red and puffy; I didn't want unnie to see me like this so I told her that I was doing homework, but I think that was a stupid excuse as unnie opened the door and came in any way she saw me sitting on my bed looking like I had cried for hours, unnie then saw that I hadn't even touched my lunch. So, she asked me if I was trying to starve myself to death because poison was a faster way, I was shocked at what she said that's when she started laughing saying that she was only joking. I smiled at her and she went and picked up my lunch from the table and kept it in front of me signalling me to open it. I opened the box and unnie fed me. It was moments like these that made me realize how lucky I was to have her. While I was eating unnie asked me if I called Minjee, I said that she hadn't answered my call so I had sent her a message. After I had finished eating unnie told me that she wanted to help me take my mind off Minjee for a day as I was continuously checking my phone to see if she had replied. I asked her what she wanted to do, she said that her friends were having a party she didn't really want to go before but she wouldn't mind taking me there so we could have some fun. I told her that she didn't have to force herself to go somewhere if she didn't want to and besides, I wouldn't really know anyone there. I thought we could just go for a movie, there were movies that would start in an hour from now but the only movie with tickets available were late in the evening. So, we just booked tickets for that movie and decided to do something else until then and somehow, we ended up deciding to pick out each other's outfit for the movie. Clothes were something that might just take my mind of Minjee, I was pulled out of my thoughts when unnie asked me if I had finished picking out an outfit from her cupboard, I was unable to decide so I told her I needed more time. I wasn't going to pick out anything normal instead I was going to surprise her with a weird outfit that she'll have no choice but to wear. Finally, I ended up picking a short green dress with puffy shoulders and beads all over it. I also chose black baggy pants and sandals, unnie was going to hate me for this she was going to look like a disaster. After my outfit was ready, I put it on hanger and left it on unnie's bed, then I headed to my room to see if unnie had finished picking outfits for me, as I went in my room my eyes went to the outfit in unnie's hand first there was no way I was going to wear that. Unnie had picked the Hanbok (Korean traditional outfit) I had worn 5 years ago for my school play and with that she had picked a green sleeve less sweater, a black bag, my black running shoes and a bath scrub? What on earth was she trying to do to me, I really didn't want to wear that so I did my best to come up with an excuse but unnie didn't want to hear it she said that she would help me put my outfit on and she would do my makeup too. I had no choice so I agreed but on the condition that I got one more chance to pick an outfit for unnie as I had gone easy unnie but she had not. Unnie told me that she would give me half an hour to pick an outfit and until then she would figure out what makeup to do for me. As soon as unnie said that I rushed out of my room, I didn't really have an outfit in mind but I had a basic image of how it would look. The first place I went to was dad's room where I grabbed his swimming trunks, a blue and white tie dyed shirt, a blue hat and a glittery red sleeve less jacket. The jacket was really shiny as it had glitter everywhere it also had 2 dolphins each on one arm, I knew unnie would hate that, she hates all things glitter. My next destination was the storage room where all my old toys were kept, I quickly opened the toy box and pulled out a paper crown, a green feather, a pair of fairy wings and some funny looking sunglasses. All I needed now was my glittery golden pants which were in my room, I checked the time there was exactly five minutes left I had to hurry and find my pants. I ran to my room and started throwing out clothes until I found it, I still had 3 minutes left so I grabbed a few make up supplies, put all of the things I had picked in a bag and rushed to unnie's room where unnie was ready and waiting for me. She asked me if I was ready, I told her that I was then unnie asked me if I wanted to get her ready first or myself. I told her that the outfit that I had picked for her was a surprise and so I wanted to go first. Unnie started by doing my makeup first she added a lot of different colours to my eyes, I felt like a rainbow. She finished my makeup by adding purple lipstick. Then she asked me to wear the Hanbok, I put it on but it was really small for me the skirt was only coming up till my knees, she then made me wear the sweater on top. With that she tied my hair into a bun and took the bath scrub and put it on my head like a hair accessory. I also had to wear socks and my black running shoes and hold a black purse I looked hideous but unnie wasn't going to look any better. Unnie took a picture of me in our backyard and then we went back to unnie's room to get her ready. Unnie had still not seen the outfit I had picked out for her, so she freaked out when she saw the mixture of clothes I took out from my bag. First, I asked unnie wear the tie died shirt and the glittery pants, on top of the shirt I made her wear the red jacket and swimming trunks, I made unnie use the paper crown as a belt and then made her wear the fairy wings. While unnie was wearing all that I took the blue hat and attached the feather to it and tied her hair into a messy bun then made her put the hat on top of the bun to cover her hair I also gave her the glasses that I had got her. I couldn't help but laugh at her. I still had to put some makeup for her; I didn't want to overdo it so I just applied some dark red lipstick. We both then went back to the backyard and I took pictures for unnie after that we went to the living room, both of us were still wearing the outfits we had picked out for each other. Unnie named my outfit 'stylish old woman' and both of us burst into giggles when the main door suddenly opened.

Chapter-8

HOME EARLY

It was dad, he had come home early. I rushed to the door with unnie behind me, dad took a good look at what both of us were wearing and couldn't hold in his laughter. He asked us what we were doing I told him we were playing dress up to which he burst into another fit of laughter. After dad had taken a seat unnie asked him if his work in Daegu was done as he had come home early, he said that his work had indeed finished early and he wanted to come back home so he booked the next flight and came back home. That's when I remembered that we had to go for a movie in less than 3 hours, but I didn't want to leave dad at home since he came early for to spend time with us so I asked him if he would like to join us, he agreed and unnie checked if we could book one more ticket luckily the seat next to ours was empty so unnie booked the tickets. Dad said that he was going to freshen up and take a little nap as he was tired from the flight and after that we could go to a restaurant and have some dinner. And until then me and unnie could go get ready. I headed to my room where all my clothes were put on the floor from when I was searching for my pants for unnie's outfit. I picked all my clothes folded them and put it back inside, even though we have maids to do all of that I feel independent doing it myself, though it took me an hour to do it. I had to get ready so I put on a pink floral dress with a matching pink shrug, grabbed a black purse, wore white converse shoes and put on some eyeshadow and Chapstick leaving the rest of my face bare. While I was putting my phone in my purse, I heard a familiar ding it was Minjee's ringtone. I quickly answered the call I was really happy she called me but she wasn't saying anything so I had to initiate the conversation I started by saying that I was sorry and asked her if she had read my message. She said she had and that she understood I was sorry but there was still a lot to talk about. I then asked her if she could forgive me, she said that she wasn't sure, she needed some time to think about it but she wants to talk to me tomorrow at school before our first class. I told her that I would meet her there and cut the call. I was happy that I had a chance to mend my broken friendship but the thing is I was also mad because if dad had got some reasonable job like a normal person, things would have not been this way. That's when unnie knocked on my door asking if I was ready to leave, I opened the door and told her that I didn't want to go, she asked me what was wrong I told her that I was mad at dad choosing to be a mafia as that's the reason Minjee is scared of me. Unnie told me that thinking like that was not right as there was a high possibility that if dad would have worked like a normal person, he wouldn't have the money to send me to such a big school and that's where I met Minjee so chances are, I wouldn't even know Minjee and I probably wouldn't have known unnie. What unnie said was right I should be thankful my dad is a mafia, maybe not thankful but I shouldn't be angry with him. I was happy I told unnie or I would have taken it all out on dad. With that me and unnie went downstairs where dad was waiting for us. It was already getting late so we left right away. We went for dinner and after we were done, we went straight to the theatre. We were 5 mins late but we didn't really miss anything but the opening and the credits. Right after the movie got over, we came back home as all three of us were tired, as soon as we reached home me and dad jumped on the couch. Unnie was really sleepy so she headed to her room while me and dad sat down and talked about what ever had happened the past 2 days, I also told him about Minjee. I told him that I was going to talk to her tomorrow and fix our broken friendship. Dad asked if she would tell the authorities, it wasn't like he could get caught that was impossible after working hard for so many years there was no way he could get caught, he had many higher authorities like the Chief of Police on his side he had a great cover up agency and everything, according to the rest of the world he owns a law firm, the irony. I told him that I wasn't sure, he asked me not to worry about it since it wouldn't cause any harm finally, we decided that it was getting late and that we both needed some rest after such a tiring day. After that me and dad were off to bed, I fell asleep as soon as my head hit the pillow.

The next day I woke up because of my alarm when I checked the phone it was already 7:20, I panicked I had to be in school by 8 o'clock to talk to Minjee, without wasting another minute I got out of bed and rushed to the bathroom where I hurried and took a bath after which I put on a grey dress shirt and black jeans, made my hair, wore the matching bracelet that I had got for me and Minjee and wore my black boots. I also grabbed my bag and put all the things I needed for school including my phone and laptop. After I made sure I was ready I rushed downstairs to look for unnie who was in the living room eating her breakfast with dad. I quickly went up to her and told her that I needed to leave, she told me to have breakfast or at least let her have breakfast. I told her that I needed to speak to Minjee before school, that's when dad said that he could drop me today since he didn't have to go to work early. Before we knew it, I was at school saying goodbye to dad, I quickly headed to the cafeteria where me and Minjee used to meet before school when I went inside, I saw Minjee standing with Suho and Jimin. I went up to her and said hi she replied and Suho did too but Jimin just backed away. I then asked her if she wanted to talk here, she said it would be better if we go to an empty classroom, I agreed and we headed to a nearby classroom. There I sat on the teachers table while Minjee and Suho sat on the bench in front and Jimin behind them. I then explained to Minjee, "You have to understand it isn't my fault that my dad is a mafia to be clear he is the boss of a big mafia group, it wasn't me who told him to get into this line of work, he made his decision way before I was born and I shouldn't be punished for his mistakes. Minjee's eyes softened hearing that but before she could say anything Jimin cut her off saying, "It's best to stay away from her, both her and her dad seems like bad news we should just report them to the officials." My eyes widened I knew that she was saying that because she was scared of me but it hurt to know that she felt that I would hurt her. It hurt more than it should have, I imagined Minjee walking out the door with Jimin never looking back what ifs filled my head like water flowing from a broken pipe, I was visibly panicked when Minjee came over to me and told me that she's not going to let go of me that easy. She only started ignoring because she thought that's what I wanted. By this time there were tears flowing, both of us crying. She also said, "I forgive you for lying I can't imagine how hard it must have been for you to live that way. I smiled through the tears to show how thankful I was that I had her. As I was sitting there wiping my tears the bell rang and the students started filing into the classroom. That's when me, Minjee and Jimin left the class saying goodbye to Suho as his class was on the other way. As soon as we got out Minjee pulled Jimin aside and told her that if anyone finds out that my dad is a mafia, she can say goodbye to her whole reputation, I don't know what went through her head but Jimin now looked like a lost puppy, she nodded her head vigorously, letting us know her lips were sealed. Jimin was terrified of Minjee and I don't blame her she can be quite scary when she's angry. Jimin swore that she wasn't going to tell anyone. I was a little worried but above all I was really happy that Minjee had forgave me. Now things would go back to normal or at least I thought.

THE END

PART 3

Chapter- 9

ANXIETY

Now I remember another reason I decided to home-school- I wasn't a morning person. I hate getting up early in the morning also it gets really cold during winters and so it's a lot harder getting up early in the morning. The sun hitting my face from the window while I try my best to keep myself warm I hate that feeling, but it's not like I have a choice anymore. With that thought I got out of bed and went to the bathroom to get ready. Once I had taken a hot shower, I changed into a hazy cable-knit turtleneck sweater with a maroon thigh length skirt, I put on Minjee and my special bracelet and I also wore the pendent unnie had gave me the day we went to grandma's house. After I was ready, I picked up my bag that I had surprisingly packed last night I also took my phone and headed downstairs to have my breakfast. After breakfast unnie dropped me to school where I met Minjee, Jimin and Suho at the cafeteria, we spoke for some time before heading to our classes. My first class for this semester was with Suho so we walked there together and then to my next class and onwards until it was time for lunch. So, as soon as the bell rang, I rushed to the cafeteria as I was starving, my stomach felt like a volcano waiting to erupt. As I got there, I looked for our table to check if anybody had already come, I saw Jimin there, I walked to her. She asked if we should wait for the others, I told her that I was starving so she could stay here and wait for Suho and Minjee while I get something for all of us to eat. I went to grab our lunches; the lunch line wasn't very long so it took me about 10 minutes to grab food for all four of us. After I got the food, I headed to the table where Jimin was and I saw that Minjee and Suho were also sitting there, I passed the food around and we all ate while talking about random things. But lunch was soon over we had to go to our classes. I went to my class and sat down on my seat, next to me my classmates sat with his mother next to him she had brought him a book he had forgotten at home. Suddenly as thoughts about mom crossed my head, I felt a splitting headache, I felt my throat burning up and I felt like the world around me was spinning, my hands were sweaty I felt like I was someone had put me in a freezer but before I could think of anything else everything went dark. The next thing I knew I was in a hospital and the IV tube was stuck to my hand with Minjee sitting next to me and as she saw me, she ran outside yelling that I had opened my eyes, she came back with a nurse and my dad. The nurse started checking my pulse and everything. When dad asked me how I was feeling, I told him that I was fine but I had a bad headache he then told me to take some rest. I then turned to Minjee and asked her what had happened, she told me that I had fainted in class so my classmate had taken me to the school clinic and then called her. The nurse at school waited for 15 mins but I kept dropping in and out of consciousness so the school called dad and rushed me to the hospital where I am right now. Minjee then told me that I need some rest so she is going to wait outside but I asked her to stay, I didn't feel good at all and I wanted her to be by my side, reluctantly she agreed, after a few minutes the doctor came in to speak to dad, after she spoke to dad she walked to the edge of my bed and asked me how I was feeling. I told her that I still had a headache she told me that they still had a few tests to do and after that if everything was alright, I could go home by tomorrow. But I didn't want to stay there for another minute, I hated being at hospitals. I didn't know why but it wasn't like I was scared I just didn't like the hospital beds or the doctors but I didn't have a choice it didn't look like they were going to let me go so I was stuck in this prison. My headache was getting worse so I tried to sleep but just as I was drifting into my fantasies, I was woken by someone banging the door. It was unnie, she was asking us to open the door which the doctor must have closed while leaving. As soon as she came in, she asked me what had happened I told her that I had just fainted and that it wasn't a big deal. I also told her that I was tired and just wanted to sleep, she said that she would leave me alone and she did and in a few minutes I had drifted off to sleep.

I woke up at around 9:00PM and turns out Minjee had left just 10 mins before I woke up, she didn't want to wake me up, so she asked dad to ask me to call her after I wake up. After I spoke to Minjee, I realised that unnie wasn't around either, so I asked dad where she was, he told me that she had some work, so she had to go home. Dad told me that I had to stay in the hospital tonight because they had to keep checking on me as after fainting I had not come back to my senses immediately and so they needed to make sure it doesn't happen again. Dad said that he would be staying at the hospital with me. He knew how much I hated being there so he thought that we could do something fun to keep me busy so I wouldn't get scared alone. I was really glad that I had such an amazing father who is always there for me, growing up without a mother has been difficult but at least I have my father by my side. As I kept thinking about dad, I realized that it had been a really long time since me and dad had spent some quality father-daughter time with each other that's why, I suggested that we stay up all night watch movies and have snacks. Dad thought for a while and said that it wouldn't be good for my health if we stay up all night so, it's better that we just watch a few movies before going to bed. I knew there was no use in arguing with him so I nodded quickly. Dad then said that he would go out and get us a few snacks for us to munch on while watching the movie. I was getting excited when the nurse bought me dinner, it was a bowl of rice, a bowl of soup and some kimchi there was also some orange juice. It didn't look too good but I couldn't stand wasting food and so, without another thought I ate my dinner. By the time I was done dad was back with the snacks, we put the snacks aside and dad sat next to me on the hospital bed while he chose a movie. We ended up watching a comedy movie and both of us couldn't stop laughing, the nurses were trying to get us to quiet down but it was no use we couldn't stop. Once we finished watching two movies dad said it was time for me to sleep, I really didn't want to sleep but I was forced to anyways so, I just lay on my bed and did my best to fall asleep. At some point I had fallen asleep but then I saw a dream where a woman was standing in front of the couch, she turned around, it was unnie she stood in front of mom whose face was turning pale I heard her scream asking for help. Mom's breathing was becoming slow and shallow and her lips were turning blue, when unnie left the room, I couldn't watch I was shaking and screaming asking someone to save her before she went limp. That's when I woke up and saw dad standing in front of my bed with two nurses as soon as I opened my eyes dad pulled me into his arms and asked me if everything was alright, I told him I was fine and that I was just having a bad dream. He seemed to understand and asked the nurses to check my blood pressure and pulse just to be sure. After the nurses had left, dad asked me if I wanted to tell him what I had seen in my dream I knew dad had just started accepting the fact that mom was gone and my dream was not going to help in anyway but I didn't want him to think I was hiding something from him. So, I told him what I had seen. But as soon as I had told him everything, I knew I should have spared the details because I was already crying and I knew dad was on the verge of crying too. His lips were trembling, and he was blinking non-stop I understood that he was doing this to hold his tears back. So, I asked him what he was thinking but as soon as his lips parted for him to speak, he started crying, I couldn't see him like that I got up and made my way to him dragging the IV tube with me, I sat next to him hugged him and both of us stayed in that position while crying together. After about 15 minutes of sitting like that I asked dad what had happened to mom, I wanted to know how she had died. Dad told me that he had no idea how mom had died other than the fact that she had consumed morphine, he said that he didn't know if she had drank the morphine on her own or if it was given to her but that didn't make sense because in grandma's house dad had said that he knew what had happened. I couldn't help but think that dad was lying to me and I didn't want go to bed pondering on that so I mustered the courage and asked him if he was lying to me because of what he told me in grandma's house he thought about it for a second and said that he isn't lying now but had lied on that day because he didn't want me to worry too much because of mom's death. He said that he didn't want me to have any pressure of finding out what had happened. So, this means he basically lied to me to make sure I don't stress myself with mom's sudden death but how could I not be stressed she was my mother, the person I needed the most and still need, I loved her, she meant the world to me. I was mad at dad but what he's saying is also right in some way he only wanted the best for me while all these things were going on in my head it was getting hard for me to breathe,

I was getting chills and I was starting to feel dizzy. It felt just like how I felt in school and at home whenever I was about to faint but only this time it was a lot stronger. I felt my heart racing just before I fainted, the next thing I knew I was in a room filled with three nurses and a doctor, the nurses were checking my IV pump and other things while the other nurse was assisting the doctor with my medical records. I got up to sit when dad asked me to lie down after the nurses were done checking me the doctor asked me how I was feeling. I told him that I was alright. He then asked me what I was thinking before I fainted, I didn't want to tell him my thoughts so I just kept quiet. He asked me if I was feeling sad or worried before I fainted, I told him that I was angry and somewhat stressed. That's when he went on to tell dad that I had anxiety, which at first was unbelievable but then the more I thought about it the more it made sense every time I fainted, I was either worried or was bothered by something. When it first happened, I was worried about how I was going to live without mom, then it kept happening when I was worried about my friends finding out about dad's work and so much more. I was always worried it was like the one thing I did best that is after crying because whenever I was in a tough situation all I ever did was cry. It was already around three in the morning at this point and I didn't think I would be able to sleep but the doctor said that he would give me a sleeping pill. Dad sat next to me on the hospital bed as the nurse handed me the pill, I swallowed it and gulped down some water after which I gently laid my throbbing head in his lap, dad stroked my hair as I fell asleep in his arms.

Chapter-10

A BIRTHDAY PARTY

The next day I woke up at noon, I could finally go back home. Dad was in the reception filling the discharge form while unnie was waiting with me. As soon as dad was back all of us went down to the parking lot. Dad took his car and unnie took hers, I got in to dad's car because unnie was going to her friend's place and I had to go home because I hadn't changed my clothes since yesterday. As soon as I reached home, I went upstairs and quickly took a shower, after I was done, I changed into a white turtle neck top with a black sweater on top, I also wore a brown checked skirt. After which I put on some simple makeup, took my bag and headed downstairs. Dad was sitting on the couch and watching TV but as I made my way to the door dad asked me where I was going. I told him that I was going to Minjee's house to plan my birthday party with her. Dad didn't really want me to go since I had just been discharged from the hospital but he didn't stop me, he said I could go but I had to be back by nine because he didn't want me to stay up too late, I promised I would be back by nine and before he could say anything else I waved at him and ran out of the door. I called the driver and asked him to come to the front of the house and that's when I realized I wouldn't have to do that by the beginning of next week, as soon as I turn 16 I am going to get my driver's license. I really loved to drive but soon I can drive legally. Just thinking about driving makes me happy but I didn't have time to enjoy that happiness as the driver had arrived and had now opened the door for me to get in. Once I was seated in the car, I wore my seatbelt and told the driver to take me to Minjee's house. On my way there I called Minjee and asked her to get ready because I was going to pick her up and we were going to go to a coffee shop so, I can tell her about everything that happened in the hospital last night. Once I reached Minjee's front door, I rang the bell and Minjee's maid opened the door she told me that Minjee was in her room getting ready and that I could go up and wait for her. I made my way to her room where Minjee was putting on makeup. The door was open so I got in, Minjee didn't realize that I had reached so I crawled from behind her and hid near her bed and when she walked over to her bed to grab her phone I jumped out and scared her. She jumped back and fell on the floor, her phone flew out of her hands and dropped screen first on the floor, I couldn't help but laugh at her and she kept scolding me from the floor. Once she had finally managed to pick herself and her phone from the floor, she asked me how I was feeling. I told her that I had anxiety and as I continued to tell her about what the doctor said she was freaking out, she asked me why I hadn't told her when I had found out. I knew I couldn't have told her over a text and I didn't want anxiety to take control of my life, I was scared but I wanted to stay strong and that's what I told Minjee. She came over to me and gave me a hug with me hugging her back, both of us not wanting to let go. After we broke the hug Minjee finished putting on her makeup while I told her everything that happened in the hospital. Once both of us were done we headed to a restaurant instead of a coffee shop because it was already time for lunch. Both of us ate lunch while trying to figure out a party location. There was a lot to do as this was my first-time planning for my birthday so late but I was so held up with school that I didn't have time and now I finally have a week off. Me and Minjee looked at many different locations until one caught my eye, it was a ballroom in a castle like house I loved the idea and I knew that my sweet sixteen will be the most unforgettable. I was now sure where I wanted to have my party, but we had to check out the ballroom first to be sure that we could host the party there. So, Minjee checked if we could have a look around before we decided on anything. The owner of the palace like house agreed to meet us in half an hour so, as soon as we were done with our lunch, we went to the house. It was absolutely stunning all the furniture and everything matched the ballroom theme. The owners of the house were an old couple they said that they live on the same road down the street and that they made this house as a holiday home for them but never really stayed there because they realized it isn't a holiday if your actual house is down the street. After we took a tour of the whole house, we let them know that we would be booking the house for an evening and that I would transfer the advance money to them by tomorrow. After we booked the venue, we headed to an ice cream parlour where we got dessert, each of us got two scoops of ice cream I got butterscotch and chocolate while Minjee got bubble gum and chocolate, after we devoured our ice cream we sat and thought of party favours. But nothing seemed to work so that was a dead end I still had to pick out an outfit for myself then there was Minjee's outfit, a DJ, the meals to be served at the party and so much more. I didn't have time and that meant I was going to be very busy for the next two weeks. After ice cream we went to my designer tailor who made all mine and Minjee's clothes for birthdays and most other events. She was a thin and tall woman in her 40s with ginger hair, she wore a white and maroon dress with a small tie. I told her my theme and she seemed to be a little too excited about it. I told her that I wanted something original as this sweet sixteen was a big deal. She told me that she would work on a few designs and send them to me by tomorrow evening which was fine with me as long as she would be able to get the dress ready in time for the party. It was already 8 in the evening by the time we were out of there I was feeling a little tired and when I told Minjee that, she said that I shouldn't tire myself as I just got out of the hospital. She would take care of the party favours if that made me feel better, I thanked her and both of us got in the car I dropped Minjee first and then headed home. After I reached home, I went to my room to change my clothes so I could lay on my bed and brainstorm a few things for the party. I put on an oversized hoodie and got on my bed I looked through a few restaurants to see which would be the best to cater for my party. I usually get the food from high end restaurants but I think this time I would hire a chef to design the menu for me. Just as I was on the phone with the caterer there was a knock on the door, I told him that I would call him back and opened the door. Unnie was standing there I asked her to come inside when unnie asked me if I had got a theme for my birthday, I told her that I had in fact figured out a theme and that I wanted to tell her and dad together. I told her to wait for me in the 2nd floor drawing room and I would get dad and join her there, dad was in his room doing something on his laptop. I knocked on his half open door and got in, he asked me if I needed anything, I told him that I had decided on a theme for my birthday and that I wanted to tell him about it. With that dad shut his laptop and both of us went to the second floor where I connected the laptop to the projector. Then I searched for the place I had booked and showed both dad and unnie the pictures while explaining the theme to them. After I had showed them the pictures and told them about the caterer, I asked them what they thought. Both unnie and dad said that it was a great idea after talking for around half an hour I told them that I had another long day ahead of me tomorrow so I needed a good night's sleep with that I said goodnight and took my leave. As soon as I reached my room I got on the bed and tried my best to fall asleep, it wasn't that hard considering the long day I had.

The next day I was awake at the crack of dawn because I had a lot to do before meeting Minjee in the afternoon. But before anything I had to get ready so I took a shower and changed into a grey shirt with blue jeans and a black sweater, I also braided my hair and put on a beanie. Once I was ready, I went downstairs for breakfast, no one else was awake and the cook had just finished preparing breakfast. So, I quickly ate my food and called my driver, as soon as the driver arrived, I got in and told him to take me to my designer. We reached the designer's boutique in no time; I got in and saw her working on something. She was wearing a long coral coloured skirt with a cream colour blouse, I went up to her and asked her if she had any good idea for my dress. She said she did, she went to the back of her shop grabbed a file and walked back, she took out a page from the file and handed it to me, it was a drawing of a off shoulder red gown it had a delicate floral lace placed on the fabric that would cover my arms. The back of the dress dipped low, while the front would be tightly fitted and embedded with soft pearls moving down before flaring out into a cathedral train which had beautifully designed flowers placed all around it. I loved the idea and loved it more when she showed me the fabric she was planning to make the gown with. It was absolutely stunning I really couldn't wait to see it come to life. I then told her that I needed the completed gown before the 13th of this month, which was in beginning of next week, she replied saying that she would do her best to get it ready by then. I thanked her and left so she could get started. My next stop was the jewellery store so I could get a tiara and a few other things. I bought a crystal tiara and earrings; I also bought a bracelet and a pendant all in red so it matches the gown. After paying for those I headed to a shoe store and bought a pair of maroon shiny stiletto heels which had a crystal wine like structure wrapped around the heel. Once I was done, I got back into the car and asked the driver to take me to a perfume store, where Minjee was waiting for me in. I reached the store I saw Minjee standing outside waiting for me, she was wearing a grey blouse with black shorts and a fur coat to top it off, I got out of the car and went to her and together we went inside the shop. Minjee told me that she had picked out a perfume that goes with my theme she showed me the design of the perfume it was in a purple antique bottle with a crystal-like lid, it looked classy and so I thought it would be perfect. I then asked her what was the fragrance that she was planning to put in those bottles, she said that she had picked out a gender-neutral fragrance which would be perfect as it could be used by everyone, I told her, "I don't know what I would do without you Minjee, Thank you.""You'd be so lost without me" she said, her lips curled up into a smile, chuckling we left the shop after ordering 100 bottles. We went to a few other stores to get the packaging for the perfumes, by the time we found the perfect packages and bought them it was already 3o'clock so we decided to take a break and have lunch. We ate fast food for lunch and then went back with our work, designing invitations and so much more.

The next few days went by without any important events, school had started so I continued shopping for my party after classes. Finally, it was the night before my birthday and I was more than excited, me and Minjee were watching a movie together but in between Minjee had gone to the toilet and for almost fifteen minutes she hadn't come back I got worried and went to look for her but the house was completely dark. I started walking to the only source of light in the house unnie's room, with each step my heart was beating faster I loved watching horror movies but I never thought I would be in a situation where I felt like the main character of a horror movie. I was now only a few steps away from unnie's room but I couldn't get myself to walk forward, my palm and forehead was covered in sweat but I had to find out what was going on. I had to end this nightmare and so I walked up to her room and slowly peeked in, it seemed like there was no one inside so I went in and suddenly the door closed behind me, and my heart gave up, everything was quiet and that's when I saw Minjee hiding behind the curtain with a cake, unnie was hiding under the bed with Jimin and dad were behind the door with Suho. I had no idea they had planned something like that, but I didn't even get a moment to think of when they had the time to plan this as they came up to me and started singing the birthday song and as soon as they were done they asked me to blow out the candles, so I did then Minjee and Suho took a handful of the cake and smeared my face with it. Now I had to wash my face so I dragged Minjee with me so I could go and get a towel to wipe my face with once I was back unnie gave me a hug and wished me after we broke the hug she said that she would be going back to sleep so it would be nice if we could all of us could leave, so we left and then dad told me that he wanted to give me my gift but it's getting late and I have a big day ahead of me so he would give it to me later and with that he kissed me on my forehead and went back to his room. After that me, Minjee, Jimin and Suho went to the home theatre and chose another movie to watch so Jimin and Suho wouldn't feel left out.

The next morning, we woke up late and had breakfast. Both Jimin and Suho left after breakfast, in sometime even Minjee had left to go get her gown and accessories. After Minjee left, I went back to my room to admire my gown, I really loved it. After which I went ahead and took out all the jewellery I bought to match with the dress and then I went to unnie's room to see what she was doing, I knocked on the door she opened it and let me in she then asked me if I had taken my medicines. I have been taking medicines since the time I had fainted and been rushed to the hospital and today I hadn't taken my medicines and so I told her that I would take them right away. She then asked me at what time me and Minjee were going to the parlour to get our hair and make-up done. I told her that we were going in a few hours that's when unnie told me that she had totally forgot about hair and make-up so I told her that I would call the parlour and book another appointment for her. She nodded in thanks and showed me her gown asking me what I thought about it, it was a white gown with a feather like fabric for the sleeves, it had a dark blue silk like material wrapped around the waist which led a large flowery lower piece. There was a tulle cape which covered the back of the backless gown. The cape had all sorts of floral designs on it. It was gorgeous so that's exactly what I told her. Unnie also showed me the floral headpiece she had bought to go with the dress, after that we spoke about the party, the guest list and a lot more. A few hours passed without any of us realising, the only thing that brought us back from our chatter was a knock on unnie's door. That meant Minjee was finally back, I told unnie that me and Minjee were going back to my room and I would call her when it was time for us to go to the parlour. Once, me and Minjee were back in my room, she hung her dress in my walk-in closet and took out all her accessories from her bag. Minjee was going to wear a skin-coloured gown which had transparent sleeves and symmetrical black lines on both sides. The front was scooped up and stopped a little above her knees, while the back was long and flowy like a wedding gown. The dress had several layers of fabrics added on top of on and another to give a simple yet rich look, the first layer of cloth that was tightly wrapped around her body was in peach colour while the materials which were layered on top of it were translucent with black glittered stripes going from side to side. She had simple black jewellery which consisted of a chocker, a watch and a pendant. As soon as Minjee had taken out all her accessories from her bag the maid came to tell us that lunch was ready so we went downstairs to eat. I didn't want to stuff myself like I usually do because I wanted to be my best self-tonight and also because I wanted to enjoy the different types of food that were going to be served today. Once Minjee had finished her lunch we went back upstairs and I asked Minjee to pack our hair accessories while I would get unnie. By the time unnie was ready we were already late so I asked the driver to hurry and drop us to the parlour, we spent almost 4 hours at the parlour. By the time we were done I looked amazing, I had full make up on, my lips painted a dark maroon while my eyes had a mix of golden and reddish making them look bigger. The heavy makeup making my cheek bones protrude, blue lens highlighting my eyes even more. My hair had been swept up in a beautiful chignon while leaving a few strands of hair to frame my face. A thick braid was pulled back and pinned to my updo. Minjee's make up was more natural with nude colours both on her eyes and lips. Her hair was tied up in a French braid tied up with different peach and black ribbons. Unnie's makeup was really thick and her hair was in a full bun with two strands of her hair in each side of her face. After all of this was done, we got back in the car but it must have taken us around an hour to get back home because of the traffic so by the time we were back home it was around 7PM. The party started at 10PM so I still had time, all I had to do now was get ready and head to the ballroom to make sure everything from the plate setting to the surprise finale was ready. I had planned a very special event that would make the night even more memorable, it's such a big surprise that even Minjee didn't know about it. I had a lot of work so as soon as we reached home, I changed into my gown and put on my gem earrings which I bought to match with my red crystal tiara. After I was fully ready, I asked Minjee to get ready quickly and headed to unnie's room to ask how much time she would take to get ready, she said that she would need some time so I told her that me and Minjee would be leaving in half an hour and if she is ready by then she should join us. She asked us to leave on our own as she was going to go pick up one of her friends and they are going to go together, I told her that the party started at 10PM so she still had time and left her room. By the time I was back Minjee was ready she looked stunning, so I told her laughing and she replied, "Thanks! You look gorgeous." As soon as we were done showering each other with compliments we went downstairs and put on our heels, mine were shimmery in a dark shade of red and Minjee had worn black heels with gems on them. Once we had put them on, we went outside and took a few pictures before we asked the driver to drop us at the ballroom. Just as we reached the ballroom I rushed to the kitchen where they were preparing the last of the dishes, I asked them if everything was going well, they replied with, "Everything is on track Miss Lee nothing to worry about" nodding in reply, I asked Minjee to check if all the decorations were in place while I checked on 'everything else' by which I meant the surprise. It took me an hour but everything was finally in place that meant me and Minjee could stuff ourselves with food and take pictures. Both of us had trays of food before we started taking pictures, we posed in the weirdest ways until one of the guards who were stationed at the door let us know that two people had already arrived early and were waiting at the door, I asked the guard if they were on the guest list, he said that they were on the list. I thought for a minute and then realized it must be Jimin and Suho so I asked the guard to let them in, in a few minutes both Jimin and Suho were in the ballroom and looking around in awe, running towards us as soon as they spotted us. Jimin was wearing a black off shoulder gown while Suho was wearing a red suit with a vest under the jacket. Jimin started the conversation by complimenting me and Minjee laughing with them as we returned the compliment. As we spoke Suho asked me why were there guards all around the place, I told him that they were all my dad's workers and they were here on dad's orders. And just as we were talking more guests started arriving one by one and with that the number of gifts on the table were increasing. As the night went by, we danced endlessly, stuffed ourselves with more food, took hundreds of pictures and talked without a break. And just as the night was coming to an end, I asked the guards to ask all the guests to gather at the terrace in 10 minutes. While I headed there first, as I reached there, I noticed that all the lanterns were placed on a beautifully decorated table waiting to be lit and blown away by the wind. Within a few minutes everyone had joined me on the terrace while Minjee walked up to me interrogating me on why everyone was in the terrace and not in the ballroom so I told her, "I've planned a surprise for everyone, I want this night to be memorable and so I bought about one hundred and fifty lanterns that we could light up and watch float away." She loved the idea and so did everyone else. Once everyone had got their lanterns and lighted them up there was a count down and at the count of one everyone let go of their lanterns. The sky was now filled with lanterns, it was absolutely extraordinary I had seen nothing quite like it so I took out my phone and asked a guard to take me, Minjee, Jimin, Suho and unnie's picture with the sky full of lanterns in the background. After the guard had taken a few pictures he handed me my phone and whispered to me in my ears asking me to check my phone after the party, I didn't get what he was trying to tell me so I just thanked him for taking the pictures and went back to admire the sky. Just as I came back Minjee told me that it was her chance to give me a surprise I asked her what she was talking about she just ignored me and took me to the parking lot where dad was standing I asked him what was going on but he wasn't giving me any answers either, both of them took me to the back of the parking lot where there was a something huge covered by a cloth looking at the way it looks and where we are right now I guessed it would be a car, dad removed the cloth and there was a very expensive car, it would easily have costed around 3,36,91,80,000 won (3 million USD). I was really confused but then dad asked me if I liked it that's when it hit me that the car was my birthday gift from dad, I was overjoyed. I hugged dad and thanked him but the hug didn't last long as Minjee said that the interior was great and that I should check it out, as I went closer, I realized the windows were open. Peeking inside I saw a case, I opened the door only to find a dog's travel case when I picked it up, I realized that there was a puppy in it; it was the cutest puppy I had ever seen. I asked Minjee which breed it was she said it was a black and tan teacup Pomeranian, I already loved him I thanked Minjee for him and she replied by saying that we were going to take turns taking care of him. I was so excited, this must have been the best birthday ever I got my first car, a puppy and had the coolest party ever. I was really excited that time flew after that, and now everyone had left. It was only me, Minjee, Suho,

Jimin, unnie and dad who were left and all of us were busy playing with Min, yup that's his name Min is the Korean word for clever and it sounds really cute so that's why I chose Min. It was already late and my dress was really heavy so I asked everyone if they were ready to leave yet and all of them answered at the same time saying that they were tired. So, we all left the ballroom with Min in my hands. Me, dad and Min got into my new car while unnie left in her car and Minjee, Jimin and Suho got a cab and left. So, it was me driving at 3am with dad next to me, and for some reason my palms were sweating I was driving dad home I never imagined a day like this, but everything went well I drove well, and the car was amazing. It was really fast which makes sense it is a luxury sports car. Once we reached home, I went upstairs to my room and the first thing I did was take off my gown put on a koala onesie, it was a little childish but it was really comfy so I put it on anyway and went to my dresser to get some make up remover, I had to take off my make up before I slept and that's what I did after which I undid my hair and brushed it to get rid of the tangles before leaving it that way. I also took out all of my accessories and put them inside, Min was already asleep on the floor so I put him on my bed and got into bed I had a long day tomorrow. As I still had to open my presents and go shopping to get pet supplies for Min, but that's when I remembered about what the guard had said in the party so I picked up my phone and looked around it I didn't get what I was meant to see so I unlocked it and checked if there was anything out of the ordinary but nothing really caught my eye that's when I had an idea I took off the case of my phone and saw a piece of paper inside. I picked it up and saw that there was something written on it, I read it out loud and it took me by surprise. It said, "Do not trust Kim Aecha, she is not who you think she is." I laughed, there was no way I would believe something that sounds like it came out of a horror movie but I had to admit I was more than a little curious on who was the one who wrote the letter and who they thought unnie actually was. I wanted to know so I went back to the note and when I looked closely, I realized that there was an address, time and a date written on it. I didn't know where the address was so I googled it and it was a nearby coffee shop, the date was on the 15th which was the day after tomorrow. They say curiosity killed the cat but it would be eating me up inside if I didn't meet this person so this means I have to go to the coffee shop at 5:30PM to find out more about the note and who had written it, but all that was for later. Right now I had to sleep and that's what I was going to do, in a few minutes, I was fast asleep.

I spent the next day opening all my presents I had got a wide range of gifts all the way from purses to a car so I enjoyed the whole day with Minjee, unnie, dad and Min. Later that day we went shopping to buy things for Min.

And finally, after a long wait it's finally the 15th there is still an hour left until I must go to the coffee shop, but I still had to get ready, so I put on a crème-coloured single sleeved jumpsuit and the new watch I got for my birthday. I added a thick black belt to it and grabbed a purse and sunglasses. I was going to leave right away because I had to meet Minjee didn't want me to go on my own, worrying about me like always she made me promise I would bring her along, at first, she thought I was overreacting but looking at how stubborn I was to go she told me she'd come along and bring along two bodyguards, dad was a mafia after all, he had a lot of enemies and they could be breaking the silent rule of not harming children and pregnant ladies to come after me. She promised to wait in the car in case I needed anything, and I happily agreed. So, as soon as I reached Minjee's house, she got in the car and both of us left to the coffee shop along with two of my dad's workers. When I parked outside the coffee shop after successfully finding it ,there was still about half an hour left until 5:30PM and I still had no idea how I was going to recognise the person who wrote the note, we waited in the car for half an hour to pass and just as I got out of the car a man bumped into me and made me drop my purse, he picked it up and handed it to me saying that all my answers were in my purse. I was more than confused but I just picked up my purse and when I turned around to thank him for picking it up he was gone I was really confused now that's when I saw that the man had left a piece of paper on my purse I took it, opened it and saw that it was a letter addressed to me along with an USB and a picture turned facing the paper in a way that I couldn't see what it contained. I held them in my hand and got back in the car as soon as I got in Minjee asked me if I had met the person, I told her what happened and so she asked me to read the letter out loud, I did as I was told. And by the time I had reached the end I was shaking and crying, never ending tears rolled down my cheeks, Minjee scooted towards me from the passenger seat and hugged me but before I could react, I had blacked out.

Chapter-11

NOTHING BUT THE TRUTH

It had been a couple of days since I had gotten the letter and I was sitting on my bed crying into Minjee's shoulder, my whole life has been a lie I didn't know who to trust anymore. Min had fallen asleep on my lap and so I couldn't move or else I would have thrown everything around again. I felt like I was going crazy but I think anyone in my place would feel the same way even though I didn't want to believe it I had to be sure I had to check the security camera but I couldn't get myself to do it, so I asked Minjee to do it but she wouldn't do it as she felt this was something only I could do. So after crying for another hour I gathered my courage and went ahead to the living room with Minjee next to me and Min following close behind doing his best catch up with those tiny legs of his as I sat down on the sofa while switching on my laptop and plugging in the USB I got with the letter. The whole time Minjee kept comforting me saying that it would be alright, as I opened the file labelled 'proof'. A shiver ran down my spine as I watched the video it was the security surveillance of the day mom passed away. It was a recording of the living room where we were sitting, mom was sitting right next to where I was sitting right now and she was doing something on her phone she looked really worried, she looked like she was talking to someone on the phone it must have been dad since she wasn't really close to any of her relatives and siblings and soon after someone walked in, they were in a maid's uniform and gave mom some tea and mom drank it and not long after her face was turning pale. At this point I knew exactly what was going on. This was exactly what I saw in my dream but there was one difference when mom was taking her last breaths, I was there I had come searching for her but when I saw her like that, I screamed for help but the maid took a cloth and covered my mouth with it and in a few seconds, I was slouched on the floor. This was it I couldn't watch anymore so I shut my laptop. I looked at Minjee and she had tears in her eyes, I was doing my best not to cry but I couldn't help it I felt unsafe just sitting at the couch I knew who the maid was and so did Minjee. I really wanted to go up to Aecha's room and slap her but there was no use in that she wasn't in her room. She was out with her friends, I couldn't call her unnie after knowing all this, that's when it hit me maybe she wasn't even my sister, maybe I was naïve enough for her to manipulate me into believing all that. I didn't know how to react to all this, I had been living with a murderer and not just any murderer it was the person who had murdered my own mother, I was really scared and I could tell Minjee was too but I knew I couldn't say anything that would make her feel better because I was just as shocked. All I knew is that I didn't want to stay at home the whole place was giving me chills I had to get out of their and so I told Minjee that we were going to get out of the house and without saying a word she followed me out the door. I grabbed my keys and got into the driver's seat while Minjee sat on the passenger's seat, we both just sat their staring out of the window lost in our thoughts not knowing what to say. The silence was broken by my phone ringing, it was dad I had to pick up but I didn't want to tell him what I had just found out, he would be furious, in one way it was my fault Aecha was still living with us. I was the one who begged dad to let her go, to let her prove her false innocence, and so I needed to figure it out on my own. I knew I had to so I just answered the call and did my best not cry. “Nay, I’m a little busy right now I just called to tell you that I’ll be staying at the headquarters tonight, there’s been an attack at a nearby warehouse and so I will have to stay here and calm everything down, please let Aecha know too, I Love you, bye.” When I heard the name Aecha I felt so tempted to tell him everything but I knew this was my own fight and so tears started streaming down my face once again, I just nodded before realising that he couldn’t see me so I just mumbled a, “Okay, love you too” and was about to cut the call but got a jab from Minjee who was sitting next to me and hearing my conversation, realising what she wanted I nodded saying, “I’m going to spend the night at Minjee’s” but my voice cracked, but he mustn't have realized so I cut the call. As soon as I cut the call, Minjee said, “I don’t think going to my house is a great idea since my aunt and cousins are over” which meant Suho and his younger siblings were there. So, we decided that we would tell Minjee’s parents that she would be sleeping over at my house so they don’t have to know that were actually staying at a hotel. We stopped at a hotel which was quite far from home but I didn’t really mind since it didn’t matter. I didn’t know what to do, all I wanted to do was make her pay but I didn’t know how. Minjee told me that the first thing we needed to do was find a way to make her confess her crime, because she had been able to hide all the evidence and managed to keep her job as a maid. Minjee was right if she went through all this to hide the evidences and kept her job meant that she has a big reason for wanting to stay back, if her aim was to kill mom then she would have just left after her job was done, but another point we were missing was that we had to know why she killed mom. There was a lot to do but we didn't know how, and so we spent that night trying to figure out what we were going to do next.

The next morning, we woke up because of my alarm for school, that's when I remembered that we were going to miss school today, but that should be the last of my concerns, even after staying up all night I have no idea how we were going to make Aecha confess and find out why she did it. The only plan we have right now is to show her the evidence we have and get her confess, but I don't think that's even a plan. We have no other option so we must work with what we have, but before all that I had to get home and be able to play it cool in front of Aecha and that's the part that frustrates me even more I don't know how I'm going to pull it off even Minjee won't be there to help me as she has to go home, it's not like I have a choice anyway. Both me and Minjee took our things, had breakfast and checked out of the hotel after which I dropped Minjee and headed home, as soon as I parked the car in the garage, I started taking deep breaths and opened the front door using my keys I didn't want Aecha to see me that is if she is still home. As I got to the stairs, I heard some noises coming from the backyard that meant Aecha was still home. I tried to hurry upstairs but it was no use she had already seen me, she called out my name, I turned to face her and as soon as I turned around, she asked me where I was, I told her that I was at Minjee's house, then she went on to ask me why I hadn't let her know of my whereabouts, I replied saying I was sorry and asked her if I could be excused. She nodded in response so I rushed to my room and closed the door behind me, in hopes that I didn't have to see her again, I was still very shaken from everything and so I didn't know what to do, I didn't know what was next. All I knew was that I wanted things to go back to normal, I have no idea how I'm going to make things go back to normal when I couldn't even save my mom. But I just have so much hatred towards her each minute I am in this house all I can wonder is why I didn't do anything to stop her from murdering my mother. But these thoughts were only going to eat me up if I didn't distract myself. I knew I couldn't stay here so I decided it was best to go to Minjee's house at least until I knew what to do next. So I grabbed a suitcase and put enough clothes for about a week, I put a few other things that I would need, closed the suitcase and made turn towards the bed when something on the desk caught my eye, it was the pendant that Aecha had given me back when we were going to grandma's house, the pendant which I had found so pretty then, now meant nothing to me I took it in my hands as I stared at it gave me chills as I felt the cold metal touch on my hand, the intertwined flowers reminded me of me and Aecha's relationship we were so different yet connected by birth, that is if the part of us being sisters is true. 'How could I be so naïve it probably isn't' I thought I wondered how much of what Aecha said to me was a lie. Questions raced my mind like a train speeding through its tracks, I had so many questions that I didn't know where to begin. For some reason fear crept over me as I continued staring at the pendant and suddenly all my thoughts started to jumble, my eyesight became weary and I broke out into a cold sweat, my lungs weren't able to take in air, I did my best to scream for help but the most that came out of my throat was a grunt I understood what was going on I was having a panic attack again and the only one who could help me right now was Aecha and just as if she could read my mind I heard her walking up to my door she opened it and saw me sitting on the floor with my legs folded towards my chest and one of my hand gripping on the pendant and the other one was holding my legs in place while my back faced the bed, she got worried at my dishevelled state. She ran towards me asking me to breath in and out at a slow pace I did my best to follow her but it was getting worse while a little oxygen continued to flow in and out my lungs it wasn't enough I felt my muscles ache begging for some more air, I felt like I was dying. Aecha saw that my condition was getting worse so she sat down in front of me and held my hand and asked me to count to ten with her. After going from one to ten almost 3 times she asked me something about Minjee to try to distract me from the fact that I couldn't breathe, but her question just made me mad and I broke; I screamed at her asking her how she could be so care free after murdering my mother but just as the words spilled out of my mouth. I saw as the colour drain from her face. It was as if she had seen a ghost, her mouth hung open and she forgot to breathe for a second as she heard her heart beat faster, and not even a moment after the words slipped from my tongue, I regretted it I didn't know what she was going to say or do next, I knew there was no taking it back but felt relieved that I could get it off my chest. After a few moments I mustered up the courage to say one word, "why" she looked at me with sorrow in her eyes and guilt written across her face and that's when she spoke but she said things that I wished I never heard. Not missing a beat since I asked the question she started talking, she said, "I don't know how to say this, I am not sure if you knew this already or not but I'm going to tell you anyway. I am really sorry but it's true I did kill your mom but I wanted to tell you exactly why though it does not justify what I did. The truth is I am not your sister from your past life I am your actual sister, your sister by birth." I had no idea what she was saying but I wasn't too shocked about the fact that she isn't my sister from my past life but her being my actual sister didn't make sense at all, at this point the tension between us was so thick it could be cut with a knife. I swallowed the lump in my throat and told her, "I want nothing but the truth." She went on saying, “my father worked as a driver to your parents he left his job about 16 years ago when he found one that paid better but the money was still not enough to run our family smoothly so he along with my mother planned to kidnap the new born daughter of his ex-boss which was your father and ask for a ransom in exchange for her, but as they bought the girl back there was a accident and she died, my parents knew that they would get killed if they didn’t return the child and so they did the next possible thing they returned you, there second daughter, my younger sister so in short you are my mom and dad’s second child while I am their first, so you’re my sister. You were born only a few days apart from the child of my fathers’ boss who you call your father, and so it wouldn’t really make a difference and as you were only a new born at the time you looked just like any other Korean new born and so your parents didn’t realize when their actual child was switched with my sister, you. A few years later my parents realized that your father was a lot richer than they actually anticipated and their greed caught up to them, so they sent me to work as a maid to keep an eye on you and try to find a way to get your mother (Lee Eon Jin), close to me so I would get some money out of her, but as I got close to your mother she found out everything and so I had no choice but kill her. My only next hope were you so I put the rebirth thing into your head already knowing the fact that your father was a mafia I changed all of my and my family’s records to match with what I had told you and got a picture online to show how you looked in you previous life. I really am sorry I only did it for my family to survive.” By this time, I was able to breathe again but my blood was boiling, “So you thought it was alright to break one family in order to make sure another doesn’t” I asked, clearly furious and cold. She looked at me with fear and shook her head saying that she never meant for it to happen. Angry, hurt, broken, lost and confused were words that couldn't even come close to expressing how I was feeling. Things had more than changed now and I didn't know what to do. It was like life was rushing ahead and I was left behind to be crushed by the stampede of people trying to make it through. Again, I felt lightheaded and in an instant the world had turned dark, for a second, I felt like I was dead I wondered if this was what death feels like, it felt quiet and peaceful but I spoke too soon I heard Aecha's voice she was screaming for help, her voice was mixed with the sound of footsteps it sounded like someone was running. They were speaking next to me yet I felt like they were really far away their voice echoed but I couldn't make out what they were saying clearly, the voices kept moving further from me until I couldn't hear anything.

After what felt like a few minutes I felt the need to open my eyes I did my best to, but it was really hard, I tried again but this time with all my might I opened my eyes but as soon as I did I wanted to close them again. My eyelids felt heavy and I was breathing fast, I tried my best to get up but the pain in my head dragged me back down, I tried again but I couldn't get up. I guess I made a lot of noise while trying to get up because I heard footsteps near me I turned my head and saw Minjee standing there, she looked at me with tears in her eyes, her eyes were red and puffy. I tried to speak to her but my voice got caught in my throat, she held my hand to assure me everything would be alright, her hand felt warm and comforting which was something I really needed right now, she told me that Aecha had told her everything, but as she said that tears rolled down her face. I was really mad at Aecha, I was at a point where anger was overflowing from my body but I didn't want to see something happen to her because I wouldn't be able to live with myself if I saw her dead because of me. It just didn't sit right with me. I could do anything to her with dad's power but I chose not to do anything on my anger. And now that I think about it all I want right now is for everything to go back to normal and I will do everything in my power to do it but these thoughts didn't linger in my mind as I was snapped out of thoughts with Minjee's voice, I turned to look at her, her eyes were still red and misty as she spoke, "Your father is on his way, are you planning to tell him everything" she asked, "I am not sure, what do you think I should do" she looked out the window for a while then said, "I already told him that you had a concussion, but I haven't told him how" I thought for a second wondering how I got a concussion, the only possible way was that I had hit my head when I fainted. But I didn't have time to think about that, dad was going to be here soon and I needed to be sure about what I was going to tell him, dad is a person who is very short tempered. He is my father after all maybe not by blood but doesn't change the fact that he loved me and cared for me as his own daughter. One thought led to another and I was now wondering if dad would still love me the same way when he finds out that I'm not actually his daughter, I wondered if he would send me back to my biological family along with Aecha, that was the last thing I would want, I wanted to ask Minjee what she thought but by the time I called for her dad had walked in, he was wearing a blue button up shirt and black jeans. There was worry written all over his face. As soon as he saw me on the hospital bed with an IV tube connected to my hand he rushed to my side asking me what had happened I told him that it was a long story and that I would tell him later, but he was really adamant to know, "I won't ask again Nayeon" I knew he wasn't joking so I asked Minjee if she could leave us alone for some time, she pressed her lips into a thin line and reluctantly nodded before she left I could clearly say she was worried but I wanted to stay strong so I held my dad's large hands and asked him to promise me that he would listen carefully and not get mad. He did as I said and then I went on to tell him everything that happened and what Aecha had told me. His expression fell making him unreadable the colour had washed out from his face, but he didn't say a word he just listened but that's what was worrying me, he wasn't showing any emotions. His eyes that showed love and affection now was a void without any emotions, his eyes resembled a black hole where a person enters but finds nothing inside. After I finished telling him everything he just got up and walked out of the room, I was too scared to even call out to him. As soon as he left the room Minjee ran into the room, she asked me what had happened I told her that I had no idea and that dad just walked out after I told him. I was worried I didn't know what was going on in his head; I wondered what he was going to do to Aecha. I was a little worried about her even though I knew I shouldn't be she had brought it upon herself, messing around with my family. Me and Minjee sat there without saying a word to each other. Doctors and nurses came and went but there was no sign of dad, I was getting really tired so I thought I would just close my eyes for a few minutes but that ended with me falling asleep. I got up with the sound of murmuring, I opened my eyes to see dad talking to a doctor, when he saw me his eyes softened, whereas I didn't know how to react I just looked down at my hands that were fiddling with my bracelet, trying to calm myself down. I have lot going on in my mind but nothing is compared to how worried I am. As soon as the doctor left dad walked towards me his face showed no emotions and as much as I wanted to move back, I kept my calm because I know my dad would never hurt me, as he walked towards me. I saw tears roll down his cheek, he went ahead to sit next to me, I held his hand in attempt to calm him down it didn't really work he just sat there sobbing while I hugged him and cried into his chest. After a few minutes he broke the silence, "So you're telling me my one and only daughter isn't mine and the only connection with my wife I had left wasn't there at all" I didn't know how to reply to that, every word he said hurt because I knew there was nothing, I could do about it. I wanted to comfort him but I couldn't all I did was cry. Dad then asked me, "I understand if you don't want to live with me and go live with your real family but I want you to know that even after all this I love you as my own daughter." I was shocked, actually shocked wasn't the word. There wasn't a word, what I was feeling couldn't be put in words. Dad was looking at me, anxious for an answer, I told him, "Firstly I would never think about leaving and secondly you're my real family and lastly I want nothing to do with Kim Aecha and her family." Dad's face lighted up it looked like the colour that had drained out was now back, and he was shining even brighter than the moon he was still crying and he said, "I'm really sorry you have to live such a complicated life all the way from your parents giving you away to live with a mafia and then killing the person you called your mother, I am really sorry that you have to go through all this but I want you to know that you are not alone and you will never be." I smiled hearing his words even after finding out that my parents killed his daughter and his wife, he cares for me. I assured him saying that he wasn't the one at fault. Now dad was back to being serious he asked me what I want to do with Aecha and her family he said that he would do whatever I ask him to do because in the end of the day they were my real parents and sister. I said, "They are dead to me but that doesn't mean I want to hurt them, I have never wanted to hurt anyone and by doing something to them I would be going against how I tried to live for so long. So, let's just forget them, let them be and go back to living the way we used to all I wish for now is for things to go back to normal, let's forget all this and live our lives." Dad smiled at me saying that he could have never wished for a better daughter, I hugged him and he hugged me back. We stayed in that position until a knock was heard on the door, I asked the person in question to come in it was Minjee, she looked at me smiling and let sighed of relief, she then said, "Aecha wants meet you, if you don't want to talk to her, I'll ask her to leave" I didn't know what to say, I looked at dad in hopes of an answer but he just shrugged so I asked Minjee to let her in. Minjee went out and was back inside in no time but this time with Aecha by her side. I didn't even feel like looking at her but curiosity was taking the best of me I really wanted to know how she had the guts to come in front of me and my dad after everything, I knew she was scared so I waited until she spoke and when she did she said, "I am really sorry for everything and I know my apologies won't change what I did, I don't know how things work in the mafia but all I am asking you is spare my parents, torture me kill me even but please leave my parents I am ready to pay for their mistakes." Her words touched my heart she could have easily put the blame on her parents saying that she's young and that she only did what she was told to do, she knows her parents were wrong but as a daughter she is ready to take the burden of their decisions, that's something I hoped to be able to do one day, give up everything I ever had for my father. I looked at her one last time letting the silence lay heavily on all of us before saying. "I would never break anyone's family apart if I had the option, I would never be able to live with myself after doing such a thing. I can see that you're hurt and sorry and that's enough for me to know that you're feeling guilty. I know that this guilt you are feeling is going to torture you more than anyone else could." I then went ahead to tell her that she was free to leave and live a happy murder free life with her parents as I wanted nothing to do with her or her family anymore, she just nodded and said, "Thank you I will be forever grateful to you and from now on my aim is to be like you, kind and forgiving." I just nodded at her and she left. Even though I didn't get the revenge I wanted I decided to be the bigger person here and let her go. Minjee walked up to me with a big smile on her face, "Let's forget all this and let things go back to normal" I tried nodding at her but I felt a sharp pain in my head and my eyes teared up that was when I remembered I was in the hospital all this stress made me forget about everything around me. Minjee saw the tears in my eyes and asked me if I was alright, I replied sarcastically, "I'm laying on a hospital bed with a concussion, I can't really move my head, I just found out that my actual sister killed the woman I called my mother and that my parents gave me up when I was a new-born, so in short my family is a lie, but I guess I'm fine." Minjee then sighed, "Aish Nayeon you're supposed to forget this ever happened" she said. But deep down I knew there was no way I would ever forget this. "I am here with the people I love most so I'm happy" I said, "Aah Nayeon why so cheesy" I got a reply. Both me and dad started laughing followed by, Minjee.

Chapter-12

HAPPILY EVER AFTER

Hey, I am Lee Nayeon, a 26-year-old living the perfect life, it's been 10 years since that day in the hospital and I haven't seen Aecha since then, it's not like I am trying to meet her but I can't help but wonder what she was doing, I stopped daydreaming when I heard a knock on my door, I asked the person to come in, it was my secretary she had come in with a few files I needed to sign, I took them from her and she left. I am the CEO and founder of my own clothing brand, which is now the second largest clothing brand in all of Korea. After I finished school, I got into fashion school in New York, while I was in my last year, I decided that I wanted to start my own business so I started taking courses on business management, fashion and a lot more and as soon as I graduated, I started my brand. I am no longer the girl who is left behind by the train of people. I am no longer crushed by the stampede of people rushing to achieve something in life. I am now walking in the front-line side by side with people who have achieved something great in life and maybe someday I'll lead them but right now I need to focus on my work. After university, Dad asked me if I wanted to be a part of his so-called business, but I declined I don't like the idea of having to kill someone for money, dad made his choice in life and I've made mine. It's not easy to get out of the mafia world while being the daughter of a world famous one. The only one rule in that line of work is that no one's allowed to mess with children or pregnant women. It's an unspoken rule but everyone follows that's how I was protected all those years but now that I'm not a child anymore a lot of dad's enemies are behind me even after I made it clear that I don't have anything to do with them, and so I learned to use a gun, I go on a few missions with dad just because I want those people out of my hair, even Minjee joins me because apparently she, 'loves the thrill of it'. Minjee has now taken over her parents' company and is getting married soon. I was yanked out of my thoughts when I heard my phone ringing, it was Minjee I picked up the call with a hello, without even wasting a minute Minjee asked me when the next mission is, I told her that she's getting married and that she should focus on that instead of risking her life for the thrill of it, she ignored me saying that I should just answer the question. I knew she wasn't going to back down now so I told her that it was tomorrow, she mumbled an okay and cut the call, laughing at her drama I put the phone down. I didn't have time to worry about tomorrow I had to go through a bunch of the new designs and decide on a final one to complete the spring collection, before I could go home. It took me the rest of the day to finish my work, it was almost midnight when I reached home, I was now living on my own. Dad had got me an apartment to stay in, the house was on the 22nd floor and it had its own garden and a beautiful view. As I unlocked the door, I felt like my body was going to faint of exhaustion, I was so tired that I didn't have the energy to even take a bath so I just changed into the first pair of pajamas I could find. As soon as I had brushed my teeth I was on my bed and fell fast asleep.

The next morning, I woke quite early at least for a weekend because I had to head to dad's headquarters by 12PM, I brushed my teeth made breakfast after which I ate it and went to take a quick shower, I then changed into a casual outfit grabbed my dress for the mission and headed out. I reached the headquarters at 11:45AM, and by 12:30PM everyone was in the meeting room discussing today's plan. By everyone I mean the seven of us, there was dad, me, Minjee and four of dads most trusted agents. One who was the inside man, his job was to sit in the headquarters and give us all the information through ear pieces we all wore. While two others were in charge of the bombs and final one was a guard. Me, Minjee and dad would be attending the gala. There's an important gala today having all the big mafia bosses attending to show off their wealth and of course dad was invited, in this event all of dad's main rivals will be present. So, we can get them all at once but the catch is that there is a strict no weapons policy, so we will have to sneak them in through different places like the kitchen, two of dads undercover agents had applied for the food supplier's job and thankfully they got it. The guards will only check the food and not the suppliers, so they will be able to get the bombs and other weapons in, and if anything goes wrong then our decoy guard will take care of it. Once we were all in, the agent will tell the undercover agents the exact locations of where the bombs must be placed while he hacks into the security cameras and shuts them off. While all this goes on me, Minjee and dad will talk to his rivals keeping them distracted so we can stall them until everything is ready. Once it is, we will shoot all of them making sure everyone else is safely escorted outside and get out of the building once all seven of us are out we'll blow the building up to make sure we get rid of all the evidence. We spent the whole afternoon going over our plan and making sure everyone is aware of our backup plans. Our backup plans had backup plans. At around 6PM we all went our ways to get ready it took me around 30 minutes to get completely ready everything from my hair to my shoes. I ran my hands down my milk white silk dress that fit snuggly around my body, the dress was extravagant, its beautifully structured cold shoulder sleeve and fitted mermaid silhouette giving it a very rich look, the dress stuck to my body like a second skin up until my waist where a bow separated the tight dress from the flowing veil like lower part. A teardrop necklace adorned my neck, matching earrings hung by my ears and a small bracelet on my wrist. I put on some simple makeup and looked at myself in the mirror one last time before I left the room, standing outside the changing room, I saw dad wearing a blue suit with a small white rose in the pocket. Dad asked me where Minjee was, I said that she was still getting ready but just as I said it, I heard the door open behind me, it was Minjee she was wearing a long Dark blue velvet dress, it had golden silver and dark blue sequins all over it, she looked like she was wearing a galaxy. Minjee had cut her hair and it was a little higher than her shoulder, highlighted her collar bone she also wore a silver metallic choker and her makeup was on point. She looked stunning but I didn't have time to tell her that, as dad told us that we had to leave now. So we rushed to the limousine our ride to the gala, the venue was in the other side of the city and the fact that dad's driver drove like a maniac didn't help, but thanks to him we reached on time. We walked into the room there was no turning back everyone was here, we spent most of the evening drinking and meeting people. Around half way through the gala I thought I was drunk because I was hearing dad's agents' voice but that's when I realized it was coming from the ear piece, he said that everyone was in their position and that we should head to the east wing of the mansion to pick up the weapons all three of us did our best to act natural and get to the east wing before I realized it. We were back with the weapons and the shootout had begun. Dad's agent had made sure that the rest of the people had evacuated the building. There was a lot of screaming and blood but it was nothing that I hadn't seen before, in about 10 minutes we had killed most of the major people but we weren't able to find our main rival the host of this party. None of us knew how she looked and we hadn't realized that until now, we didn't really have time to find out because who it was as the guards had gotten hands on a few weapons and they started shooting back we did our best to dodge them but one hit Minjee's arm at that point both dad and me knew it wasn't worth it anymore, Minjee was bleeding and finding the host was the last thing on our minds, we knew we had to get out and blow this place up. I did my best to shoot down all the guards and cover dad while he was trying to get Minjee out of the mansion. As soon as we were out of the mansion and near our limousine, the agent clicked on the button and right before our eyes the whole building erupted into flames.

A month had passed since the last mission and Minjee has heeled fully since the bullet didn't go that deep. Dad's team is doing their best to find out who the host was, but the only thing they found out is that she would be making a special appearance in tomorrow's party, there was a party for a very famous hitman's daughter's birthday and our target was going to be the guest of honour. We've been preparing for since the last two weeks, the problem is that we have to make sure we don't hurt any children in the process so we planned to lure her out in between the party and then finish her but it's not going to be easy since she is the guest of honour and everyone would want to meet her. But we had to try because we didn't know when we'd get such an opportunity again. After she was dead I could sleep peacefully again, I won't even have to touch a gun again.

It was finally time for the party Minjee insisted on coming saying that this would be her last mission before her wedding and I knew she was right and there was no way she was going to change her mind now. Minjee held on to my hand in excitement as we entered the hotel where the party was taking place. We walked around the place while we waited for the guest of honour to be introduced, after almost half an hour the birthday girl's father asked for everyone's attention when everyone had turned towards him, he said that the guest of honour was here so me and Minjee walked to the front to take a closer look while dad followed us. Just as we took our places near the entrance, I crossed my fingers in hope that this will be my last mission and I can live in peace after this. The door opened in front of me and a number of guards walked behind whom stood a woman in a knee length pastel coloured single sleeve dress, I didn't understand why she needed to have such a dramatic entrance, but as soon as she turned around I realized that she deserved such an entrance, I couldn't believe my eyes, she looked the same yet very different, my brain went into overdrive had stopped functioning because of the amount of questions I had, my nerves had stopped sending signals to my brain I thought I would get a panic attack, in the blink of an eye the tables had turned. Minjee was just as shocked as I was, she kept repeating that it must be a mistake but our doubts were cleared right away when the hitman said, "Please welcome Kim Aecha, Seoul's biggest female mafia leader."

THE END

www.ingramcontent.com/pod-product-compliance
Ingram Content Group UK Ltd.
Pitfield, Milton Keynes, MK11 3LW, UK
UKHW041843200726
13854UKWH00005BA/2044

9 789393 809773